# WICKED VELOCIRAPTORS
# OF
# WEST VIRGINIA

### Here's what readers from around the country are saying about Johnathan Rand's AMERICAN CHILLERS:

"I just read Terrible Tractors of Texas, and it was great! I live in Texas, and that book totally freaked me out!"
-Sean P., age 9, Texas

"I love your books! Can you make more so I can read them?"
-Alexis B., age 8, Michigan

"Last week, two kids in the library got into a fight over one of your books. But I don't remember what book it was."
-Kylee R., age 9, Nebraska

"I read The Haunted Schoolhouse in three days, and I'm reading it again! What a great book."
-Craig F., age 12, Florida

"I got Invisible Iguanas of Illinois for my birthday, and it's awesome! Write another one about Illinois!"
-Nick L., age 11, Illinois

"My brother says you're afraid of the dark, which is silly. But my brother makes things up a lot. I love your books, though!"
-Hope S., age 9, California

"I love your books! Make a book and put my name in it. That would be sweet!"
-Mark P., age 10, Montana

"Your books give me the chills! I really, really love them, but I don't know what one I like best."

-Jeff M., age 12, Utah

"I was read WISCONSIN WEREWOLVES, and now I'm freaked out, because I live in Wisconsin. I never knew we had werewolves."

-Angie T., age 9, Wisconsin

"I have every single AMERICAN CHILLER except VIRTUAL VAMPIRES OF VERMONT. I love all of them!"

-Cole H ., age 11, Michigan

"The lady at the bookstore told me I should read NEBRASKA NIGHTCRAWLERS, so I did. I just finished it, and it was GREAT!"

-Stephen S., age 8, Oklahoma

"SOUTH CAROLINA SEA CREATURES is the best book in the whole world!"

-Ashlee L, age 11, Georgia

"I read your books every night!"

-Aaron. W, age 10, New York

"I love your books! When I read AMERICAN CHILLERS, it's like I'm part of the story!"

-Leroy N., age 8, Rhode Island

"KREEPY KLOWNS OF KALAMAZOO is my favorite. It was awesome! I did a book report about it, and I got an 'A'!

-Samantha T., age 10, Illinois

"I'm writing to tell you that THE MICHIGAN MEGA-MON-STERS was the scariest book I've ever read!"

-Clare H., age 11, Michigan

"In class, we read FLORIDA FOG PHANTOMS. I had never read your books before, but now I'm going to read all of them!"

-Clark D., age 8, North Carolina

"Our school library has all of your books, but they're always checked out. I have to wait two weeks to get OGRES OF OHIO. Can't you do something about that?"

-Abigail W., age 12, Minnesota

"When we visited Chillermania!, me and my brother met you! Do you remember? I had a red shirt on. Anyway, I bought DINOSAURS DESTROY DETROIT. It was great!"

-Carrie R., age 12, Ohio

"For school, we have to write to our favorite author. So I'm writing to you. If I get a letter back, my teacher says I can read it to the class. Can you send me a letter back? Not a long one, though. P.S. Everyone in my school loves your books!"

-Jim A., age 9, Arizona

"I LOVE AMERICAN CHILLERS!"

-Cassidy H., age 8, Missouri

"My mom is freaked out by the cover of POISONOUS PYTHONS PARALYZE PENNSYLVANIA. I told her if she really wanted to get freaked out, read the book! It's so scary I had to sleep with the light on!"

-Ally K., age 12, Tennessee

*Don't miss these exciting, action-packed books by Johnathan Rand:*

## Michigan Chillers:

#1: Mayhem on Mackinac Island
#2: Terror Stalks Traverse City
#3: Poltergeists of Petoskey
#4: Aliens Attack Alpena
#5: Gargoyles of Gaylord
#6: Strange Spirits of St. Ignace
#7: Kreepy Klowns of Kalamazoo
#8: Dinosaurs Destroy Detroit
#9: Sinister Spiders of Saginaw
#10: Mackinaw City Mummies
#11: Great Lakes Ghost Ship
#12: AuSable Alligators
#13: Gruesome Ghouls of Grand Rapids
#14: Bionic Bats of Bay City

## American Chillers:

#1: The Michigan Mega-Monsters
#2: Ogres of Ohio
#3: Florida Fog Phantoms
#4: New York Ninjas
#5: Terrible Tractors of Texas
#6: Invisible Iguanas of Illinois
#7: Wisconsin Werewolves
#8: Minnesota Mall Mannequins
#9: Iron Insects Invade Indiana
#10: Missouri Madhouse
#11: Poisonous Pythons Paralyze Pennsylvania
#12: Dangerous Dolls of Delaware
#13: Virtual Vampires of Vermont
#14: Creepy Condors of California
#15: Nebraska Nightcrawlers
#16: Alien Androids Assault Arizona
#17: South Carolina Sea Creatures
#18: Washington Wax Museum
#19: North Dakota Night Dragons
#20: Mutant Mammoths of Montana
#21: Terrifying Toys of Tennessee
#22: Nuclear Jellyfish of New Jersey
#23: Wicked Velociraptors of West Virginia

## Freddie Fernortner, Fearless First Grader:

#1: The Fantastic Flying Bicycle
#2: The Super-Scary Night Thingy
#3: A Haunting We Will Go
#4: Freddie's Dog Walking Service
#5: The Big Box Fort
#6: Mr. Chewy's Big Adventure
#7: The Magical Wading Pool

## Adventure Club series:

#1: Ghost in the Graveyard
#2: Ghost in the Grand
#3: The Haunted Schoolhouse

## For Teens:

PANDEMIA: A novel of the bird flu and the end of the world
*(written with Christopher Knight)*

# #23: Wicked Velociraptors of West Virginia

# Johnathan Rand

# An AudioCraft Publishing, Inc. book

This book is a work of fiction. Names, places, characters and incidents are used fictitiously, or are products of the author's very active imagination.

Book storage and warehouses provided by Chillermania!©
Indian River, Michigan

Warehouse security provided by:
Lily Munster and Scooby-Boo

American Chillers #23: Wicked Velociraptors of West Virginia
ISBN 13-digit: 978-1-893699-94-6

**Librarians/Media Specialists:**
PCIP/MARC records available **free of charge** at
www.americanchillers.com

Cover illustration by Dwayne Harris
Cover layout and design by Sue Harring

Printed in USA

# Wicked
# Velociraptors
# of
# West Virginia

# VISIT CHILLERMANIA!

*WORLD HEADQUARTERS FOR BOOKS BY JONATHAN RAND!*

Yooperland

Indian River

Alpena

Traverse City

**MICHIGAN**

Mt. Pleasant

Bay City

Grand Rapids

Lansing

Detroit

Kalamazoo

**CHILLERMANIA!**

*I-75 Exit 313
then south
1 mile!*

Visit the HOME for books by Johnathan Rand! Featuring books, hats, shirts, bookmarks and other cool stuff not available anywhere else in the world! Plus, watch the American Chillers website for news of special events and signings at *CHILLERMANIA!* with author Johnathan Rand! Located in northern lower Michigan, on I-75! Take exit 313 . . . then south 1 mile! For more info, call (231) 238-0338. And be afraid! Be veeeery afraaaaaaiiiid . . . .

# 1

"Ready?" Kara asked me.

"Go for it," I said, stooping forward and holding the baseball bat over my shoulder. "I'm going to knock this one into next week!"

It was Saturday, and my friend Kara Haynes and I were practicing hitting a softball. Actually, *I* was the one working on my hitting. I think I'm a pretty good player, but the coach wanted me to work on my swings. He said I could be really good if I could hit the ball a little farther.

As for Kara? She didn't need to work on her hitting or pitching. She's the only girl on the team, and she's really good. When it comes to softball, she can hit, run, and pitch. In fact, she's the team's starting pitcher. She's ten times better than any of the guys, and that makes some of them jealous.

Not me, though. I'm just glad she's my friend, and she's willing to help me.

Midnight, my black Labrador, sat in the grass near the side of the road. We adopted him from an animal shelter last year, and he's the best dog in the whole world. He's really smart, and I include him as one of my best friends. Everywhere I go, Midnight goes. Except for school, of course.

Kara let the ball fly. As usual, her pitch was perfect. I swung as hard as I could . . . but the bat only skimmed the bottom of the ball, causing it to pop up into the air and arc down behind me. It bounced a couple of times, then rolled down the street.

"Midnight!" I shouted. Without saying anything more, Midnight leapt into action, chasing after the softball.

"You need to loosen up, Brandon," Kara called out. "You're too stiff. Let the bat flow with your body."

Easy for *her* to say.

The softball took a bounce over a curb and into the grass. Midnight snapped it up in his jaws while it was still rolling. He trotted back to me, dropped the ball into my hand, and sat.

"Good boy," I said, patting his head. "Go lay down." Midnight stood and walked to the side of the road where he laid down again, ready to chase the ball.

I paused for a moment to look around. Here, near the end of our block, there weren't very many houses. That's why it was a good place to practice hitting: there wasn't much danger of hitting anything or anyone. Sure, it would be a lot better if we could practice at the softball field, but the closest one was ten miles away. Kara lived on the same block I did, so it was a lot easier and more convenient to hike to the end of the block and practice.

She was still standing in the middle of the road with her right hand on her hip. Her left hand, covered by a worn, leather softball glove, hung at her side. Her glossy black hair shined in the late morning sun, and she was squinting as she watched me.

"Did you hear what I said?" she asked.

"Yeah," I replied. "You said I need to loosen up."

"You can still swing hard," she said, "just try not to be so tense. And be sure to follow through with your swing." She grasped an invisible bat and demonstrated by making a slow swing.

"Let's try again," I said, tossing the ball to her. She snapped it out of the air with her glove.

"You'll get it," she said. "Just keep your eyes focused on the ball, and stay loose."

I pulled the bat over my right shoulder and spread my feet.

"Loosen up your shoulders," Kara said. "You need to be comfortable."

Now that Kara mentioned it, I noticed my shoulder muscles were really tight. I relaxed a little and took a deep breath.

"That's it," Kara said, winding up. "Here it comes."

*And here it goes,* I thought. *I'm going to really nail this one.*

She threw the softball, and I swung. The bat

connected with a solid *thwack!* and the softball went flying.

"That's the way!" Kara shouted as the ball soared high over her head. I don't think I'd ever hit a ball so hard or so high. It sailed over the treetops and vanished.

*"Holy crow!"* I shouted. *"That's a home run if I ever saw one!"*

My elation and excitement, however, were short lived. Seconds later, we heard the distant, piercing sound of shattering glass. Midnight flinched and let out a single, startled bark.

I dropped the bat, and it clunked to the pavement.

*Oh, no,* I thought. *This isn't just bad. This is terrible. A disaster.*

You see, it was bad enough I'd broken a window . . . but what made matters worse was the fact that the only home in that direction belonged to none other than Dr. Joseph Wentmeyer.

And everyone knew that not only was Dr. Wentmeyer a mean person, he was also crazy as a loon.

I had broken his window, and I would have

to face him. I was scared to even get *close* to his house, let alone have to speak with him.

Now, however, as I look back, facing Dr. Wentmeyer wasn't the worst part. Oh, it was bad, all right. You see, if I hadn't broken the window, I wouldn't have had to face Dr. Wentmeyer . . . and I wouldn't have had to face the velociraptors.

Breaking a window was bad enough.

Breaking Dr. Wentmeyer's window made it much worse. Sure, it was an accident. I never imagined I would have been able to hit the ball far enough to reach his house. His home wasn't even visible from where we were, because there was a line of thick trees that grew all around it. It was as if they were planted on purpose, to hide the house from the outside world.

"Uh-oh," Kara said. "That's not good."

"You can say that again," I said. I felt like

crawling into a hole. Once, I accidentally broke a window in our house. Dad and Mom were mad, but it had been an accident, and I didn't get into too much trouble.

Breaking someone else's window, however, was a different story.

"I've got to tell Dr. Wentmeyer I was the one who broke his window," I said glumly. I picked up the bat. "Come on, Midnight."

Midnight got to his feet, shook, and trotted up to me with his tail wagging.

"I'll go with you," Kara said. "After all, it's my fault, too. If I wasn't such a good pitcher, you would never have hit the ball as hard as you did."

I smiled. Kara wasn't bragging; she was only being funny. Besides: she really was a great pitcher.

We walked down the street, and I must say I wasn't in any hurry. I wasn't looking forward to confronting Dr. Wentmeyer. I'd never spoken to him before, and the only things I knew about him were what my friends and classmates had told me.

At his driveway, we stopped. His three-story house loomed up, and it seemed to become part of the sky and trees. A black iron gate was open, but the fence continued around the property to keep people out. There were signs posted that read 'KEEP OUT!' and 'NO TRESPASSING!'

"Looks like Dr. Wentmeyer is a real friendly guy," Kara said.

"Yeah," I said. "And he's going to be even friendlier when he finds out I broke one of his windows."

"I don't see anything broken," Kara said. "Maybe you didn't break a window."

"Oh, I'm sure it was a window," I said. "But the ball would have dropped over there." I pointed. "It probably hit a window on the other side of his house. Come on." I started up the driveway.

"But his signs say he doesn't want anyone trespassing," Kara said.

"Yeah, but this is different," I said. "We're not trespassing. We're coming to tell him we broke one of his windows. It would be worse just to leave and not say anything about it."

I walked up the driveway with Midnight at my side. Kara followed.

"It sure looks like a lonely place," Kara said. "And it doesn't look like he's home."

We stepped onto the porch. The front door was solid wood, with a brass doorknob and knocker. I reached out and rapped several times. We listened for any sounds from within the house, but there were none.

I rapped several more times.

Still, Dr. Wentmeyer didn't come to the door.

"He's probably not home," Kara said.

"Let's walk around to the other side of the house," I said as I stepped off the porch. "Let's see if we can find the broken window. If Dr. Wentmeyer isn't home, we can leave him a note."

We strode around to the other side of the house. Sure enough, we found a broken window. It was on the first floor, and there was a distinct hole in the glass where the softball had hit. Pieces of the window had broken out, and a few of them had fallen to the grass.

"Sit, Midnight," I said, and he obeyed. I didn't want him stepping on glass and cutting his paws.

I walked to the window, mindful of the glass at my feet.

"I think the ball must have gone into the house," I said. "I don't see it anywhere."

There were no curtains on the window, and I decided to peer inside to see if I could spot my softball. I knew I shouldn't, because it was like spying or something. But I had to know. Maybe the ball had hit Dr. Wentmeyer. That would be awful. Or the ball might've broken something inside. That would be bad, too.

I stood on my tiptoes and looked inside.

I didn't see my softball . . . but what I *did* see made me gasp.

*"Kara!"* I exclaimed. *"Come here! You've got to see this!"*

Kara came to my side and peered through the window.

"Be careful," I said. "Some of the broken glass is loose."

"What *is* all that stuff?" she asked.

"It looks like a laboratory or something," I replied.

There were no lights on in the room, but we could see all sorts of electrical equipment, test tubes, and beakers on several desks. Papers and books were stacked in disheveled piles on the floor and on tables. My bedroom gets messy once in a while, but nothing like this. This place was a pig pen.

*"This must be where he does his experiments,"* Kara whispered. *"What kind of doctor is he?"*

"A mad doctor," I said. "At least that's what all my friends say."

"He must be some sort of inventor or scientist," Kara said. "My dad is a doctor, and he doesn't have anything like this in our house. My mom would have a fit if we had a mess in our house like this."

I spotted my softball.

"There's the ball, right over there," I said. "On the floor, by that table over there."

"At least it didn't break anything in the room," Kara said. "The window is bad enough, but some of this stuff looks really expensive."

"Dr. Wentmeyer?" I called out. "Are you home?"

We listened, but the only things we heard were a whisper of wind in the trees and a few birds chirping.

"Dr. Wentmeyer?"

Still nothing.

"He's not home," Kara said.

I was relieved. I didn't want to have to face Dr. Wentmeyer and tell him we broke his window. Sure, I'd have to confront him sooner or later. But I was able to put it off for the time being.

"Let's leave him a note," I said. "We'll have to go home first and get some paper."

I stepped back from the window, and Kara did the same.

"Well," she said as she patted my back. "Look on the bright side. You *really* smacked that ball. You're getting better."

"We're going to have to find somewhere else to practice," I said. "I never thought I'd be able to hit the ball that far."

Midnight saw us walking away and stood.

"Come on, bud," I said. He shook, wagged his tail, and followed us as we walked around to the front of the house.

Suddenly, we heard the sound of tires on pavement. A car was approaching, but we couldn't see it through the thick trees and black fence.

But when it turned into the driveway, my

heart leapt into my throat. Blood rushed to my face. I felt hot.

The car was all black, and it prowled up the driveway like a panther. Kara and I stopped walking. Midnight stopped at my side and let out a low growl.

The car halted. Still, we couldn't see through the windows. The glass reflected the sky and the trees. It was like looking at mirrors.

The driver's side door opened.

A black shoe emerged and stepped onto the pavement. Then another.

Dr. Wentmeyer had come home.

# 4

Until now, I'd only seen Dr. Wentmeyer from a distance. He always wore black pants, a white shirt, black shoes, and glasses with black rims. His hair was gray and messy. He never smiled.

And he wasn't smiling now, either.

He stood, and he was much taller than I expected. Like usual, he was dressed in black pants and a white shirt. His gray hair tossed in the breeze.

"And just *what* are you doing here?" he snarled. "Can't you read the signs?"

Kara and I didn't say a word. Midnight, who is usually very friendly toward other people, continued to growl softly. I patted his head.

"What's the matter?" Dr. Wentmeyer sneered. "Cat got your tongues?"

I spoke. "We . . . we were . . . um, uh—"

"You were *trespassing*," Dr. Wentmeyer interrupted. "I think I'm going to call the police. I'll ask you again: what are you *doing* here?"

"We accidentally broke one of your windows with a softball," Kara blurted out.

"I did it," I said. "I was the one. I hit the ball."

Dr. Wentmeyer looked furious. "You broke a window?!?! *You broke a window?!?!*"

"It was an accident," I pleaded. "I didn't do it on purpose. I never thought I'd be able to hit the ball as far as I did."

"Show me the window you broke," Dr. Wentmeyer said. His voice trembled with anger, and I knew I was in a lot of trouble. More trouble than I'd even imagined.

I pointed. "It's over there, on the other side of the house."

"I didn't say 'point,' boy. I said take me there."

Things were not looking good. If Dr. Wentmeyer was angry now, he was going to go ape-crazy when he saw the broken glass all over the ground and inside his house.

Kara and I turned and led the doctor to the back of his house. Midnight had stopped growling, but the hair on his back stood up. He didn't like the tall, strange man with the messy hair.

When we reached the window, I pointed to the glass on the ground. Then, I pointed to the window.

"It was an accident, honest," I said. "I didn't mean to break it."

"That's why we came to your house," Kara explained. "We wanted to tell you we were the ones who broke your window."

Dr. Wentmeyer peered through the window. "There doesn't seem to be anything broken inside," he said. Then, he turned and looked at us. He didn't seem quite as angry as he had been. "Well, I don't think I'll have to call the police, since you were only doing the right thing. But you'll have to pay for the window."

Gulp.

"How . . . how much will it cost?" I asked.

"Fifty dollars," Dr. Wentmeyer replied.

*"Fifty dollars!?!?"* I said. "Holy crow! I don't have that much money!"

Kara shook her head. "Neither do I," she said.

"That's not my problem," Dr. Wentmeyer said. "You broke my window. You'll have to find a way to pay for it. Unless . . . ."

He stopped speaking and looked at the fragments of glass in the grass. "Unless you would like to work it off. Yes, yes . . . now *there's* an idea."

He turned and looked at us. Again, I was shocked at how tall he was. "How are you at mowing lawns and picking up brush? Can you wash windows?"

I looked at Kara, and she looked at me. Then, I looked at Dr. Wentmeyer.

"I mow our lawn at home with Dad's push mower," I said. "And I can pick up sticks and things."

"Me, too," Kara said, bobbing her head.

"Well, then," the doctor continued, "perhaps we can make a deal. The grounds around my private laboratory are in need of attention. If you will mow the lawn, pick up sticks and branches, and wash the windows on the outside, I would say that would be worth the price of the window you broke. Could you do that?"

Again, I looked at Kara, and she looked at me. We really didn't have any choice, since neither of us had any money.

"Yes," we both said at the same time.

For the first time, Dr. Wentmeyer smiled. "Good," he said. "My laboratory is only a mile away. I'll give you directions, and you can get to work in the morning. Fair enough?"

We nodded.

"Good," the doctor said with a sly smile. "I'll see you in the morning, then."

*Cool,* I thought with a huge sense of relief. *I only have a few dollars in my bank at home. It would take me ten years to pay Dr. Wentmeyer for the broken window.*

I didn't know what to expect when we got

to his laboratory, but I'll say this much: when Kara and I arrived the next morning, we could only stare . . . and wonder what we'd gotten ourselves into.

After we left Dr. Wentmeyer's house, I went home and told my mom and dad that I'd accidentally broken his window. I thought they were going to be mad, but they weren't. Actually, Dad said I did the right thing by owning up to my responsibility. He said everyone makes mistakes, and it's important to fix them.

The next morning, Kara and I rode our bicycles to Dr. Wentmeyer's laboratory. Midnight followed close behind, every once in a while darting to the side of the road to sniff something.

Dr. Wentmeyer's laboratory wasn't very far, but I'd never seen it before because it was at the end of a long road. There were no other homes around. The only thing we could see was a black iron gate—just like the one Dr. Wentmeyer had at his house. And, just like his home, there were several 'NO TRESPASSING' signs posted on the fence. There were also several small security cameras mounted on either side of the gate. On the other side, we could see a large, single-story building in the distance.

"Well, we're here," I said. "I'll see if the gate's locked."

I got off my bike and walked to the gate. Flapping wings drew my attention above, and I saw three crows flying. The sky was clear, except for a few puffy white clouds.

As I expected, the gate was locked. But when I let go of it, I heard a click and a buzzing sound. He had probably been watching for us through the security camera and had opened the gate by remote control.

The gate swung open, and we could see the building in the distance.

"*That's* his laboratory?" Kara asked.

"It must be," I said.

We stared. The building was huge, and it had an enormous lawn. The grass was six or seven inches long! It looked like it hadn't been cut all summer.

And there were dozens of windows, too. We were too far away to see how clean—or dirty—they were, but I knew Kara and I had our work cut out for us. This wasn't going to be a job that would take only an hour or two. This was going to take us all day . . . maybe longer.

"*Holy crow,*" I breathed. "*This is going to take forever.*"

"Then let's get started," Kara said.

I hopped on my bike, and we pedaled down the long driveway. Midnight padded along behind us. When I turned to check on him, I saw the gate had already closed.

And as we drew closer to the large laboratory, we could see that the black iron fence went all the way around the property.

"This guy really wants to keep people out," I said. "I wonder what he's working on in his laboratory."

"It must be something he wants kept a secret," Kara replied.

We pedaled up to the building and stopped our bikes near Dr. Wentmeyer's black car. There were no other vehicles around, and I figured the doctor probably worked alone. Again, I wondered what he was working on his laboratory.

"Maybe he's working on a top-secret project for the government," I said as I hopped off my bike.

"Or maybe he's creating a vaccine for some disease," Kara said.

All of a sudden, we heard a loud explosion from somewhere inside the building . . . followed by the hollow sound of a man screaming!

The blast was so loud, the ground trembled. We flinched in surprise, and Midnight jumped.

*"What was that!?!?"* Kara asked.

"Something blew up!" I replied.

"No kidding," Kara said. "I wonder what it was."

"And that scream had to have been Dr. Wentmeyer!" I said. "Come on! We've got to get inside and see if he's okay!"

We raced to two large, steel doors, only to find them locked. I darted to one of the windows.

It was locked, too, and there was a curtain drawn on the inside so I couldn't see in. Stepping back from the building, I noticed all the windows were like that.

"Maybe there's a back door," Kara said.

"Let's find out," I replied. We ran across the thick, unmown lawn, and around to the side of the building. Midnight followed. We saw more windows, but they all had curtains drawn.

At the back of the building, we found another set of steel doors. Like the front doors, they were locked.

"We should tell someone," I said. "Dr. Wentmeyer might be hurt. That was a big explosion."

We ran around to the front of the building. I was really worried about Dr. Wentmeyer. Sure, he might be a little nutty, but that didn't mean I wanted any harm to come to him.

But if we couldn't get in, how would we know if he was okay or not?

"Let's go," Kara said. "We can ride our bikes back to my house and call for help."

That sounded like the best thing to do. We

had no idea what had happened inside Dr. Wentmeyer's laboratory, but we'd heard a loud explosion . . . and a scream. *Something* had happened, that was for sure.

I hopped on my bike. "Come on, Midnight," I said, and he galloped up to me, wagging his tail. Kara got on her bike.

"Wait a minute," I said, pointing to the gate in the distance. "We're locked in. We can't go anywhere."

And that's when we heard another noise.

The front door opened.

We turned and stared.

Dr. Wentmeyer stood in the doorway, and, by the looks of him, something had gone horribly wrong in his laboratory.

**7**

Dr. Wentmeyer looked frazzled. His hair looked even more messy than normal, and there were streaks of black soot in it. His white shirt had dark char marks on it, and it was torn in several places. Swaths of black grease blotched his arms, hands, and face. There was a large rip in his pants, just below the knee. One of his shoes was missing, and his glasses were askew. And he was staring at us with a confused look, as if he were in a daze.

Kara and I could only stare. Something had gone seriously wrong, I was sure.

Finally, I spoke.

"Are . . . are you all right?" I asked.

Dr. Wentmeyer didn't reply. He just stared and blinked his eyes a few times.

"Dr. Wentmeyer?" I said.

Suddenly, a grin began to form on his face. His lips parted, and I could see his teeth. He slowly raised one fist into the air.

"Success!" he exclaimed. "After years and years of work—success! I've finally done it!"

"What have you done?" Kara asked. "We heard something blow up."

"My invention is finally complete!" Dr. Wentmeyer said. He clasped his hands together. "I've done it! Everyone told me it couldn't be done, but I've proven them wrong! I've done it! I've done it!"

Then, he began hopping up and down like an excited child. He looked funny—especially since he was supposed to be mean and crazy. Well, maybe he was a little crazy, but the person we were now seeing didn't look like he had a mean bone in his body.

And he only had on one shoe, so he *really*

looked silly, hopping up and down like he was.

"What did you invent?" I asked.

"I've invented a time machine!" he said. He stopped jumping up and down and suddenly realized he was missing a shoe. He looked around his feet for a moment, then behind him. He didn't find his shoe, and he seemed to forget about it when he faced us again.

"A time machine?" Kara asked.

"Yes, a time machine," Dr. Wentmeyer replied. "It's my life's work! This could be the most important invention in all of history!"

Kara looked at me and rolled her eyes. I could tell she didn't believe a word Dr. Wentmeyer was saying.

"You mean you've made a machine that can travel through time?" I asked him. I'd read books and watched movies about time travel, but they were just made up stories. I didn't think time travel was possible.

"Precisely!" Dr. Wentmeyer replied.

"But what was that explosion we heard?" Kara asked.

"A mere mishap," the doctor replied. "No

harm done. The important thing is that my time travel machine is perfected!"

He reminded me of a little kid on his birthday. I've never seen a grown-up so excited about anything.

"Would you like to see it?" the doctor asked.

Kara shot me a quick glance and mouthed the word *no* . . . but it was too late: the word 'yes' had already left my lips.

"Follow me," Dr. Wentmeyer said, and he turned and walked into the building.

"Can I bring my dog?" I asked.

"Certainly!" Dr. Wentmeyer said without turning around.

Kara and I got off our bikes.

"Come on, Midnight," I said as we walked toward the big steel doors.

"We're going to be sorry," Kara said quietly.

"We'll be fine," I said. "Besides: I'm really curious to see his invention."

Kara shook her head. "I don't think this is a good idea," she said.

"All we're going to do is take a look at his invention," I said. "What could possibly go wrong?"

Well, lots of things could go wrong—and they were about to.

When we walked through the front doors of the building, it was like walking into a cluttered flea market. We were in a big hallway that looked like it stretched the entire length of the building. The floor was a stale white tile, and the walls and ceiling were a pale gray. Bars of white fluorescent lights illuminated the hall. There were all sorts of odds and ends everywhere. Everything from old televisions and radios, satellite dishes, microwave ovens, toasters, blenders, coils of wires and cables, books and newspapers and magazines all piled on top of one another. Nothing seemed to be organized, and most of the electrical appliances had been partially taken apart. It was like a tornado had struck a garage sale.

*"Dr. Wentmeyer sure doesn't keep a tidy place,"* I whispered as we walked. *"This is as bad as the room we saw at his house."* Behind me, Midnight was pausing to sniff a few items strewn about.

*"If my room looked half this bad, my parents would ground me for a year,"* Kara said quietly.

Ahead of us, Dr. Wentmeyer was walking down the long corridor, with one shoe clacking on the tile. There were doors on both sides, and they were all closed. Some of them had windows with wires that crisscrossed through the glass. There were no lights on in these rooms, and we couldn't see inside.

The doctor was talking, but we were too far behind him to hear what he was saying. We walked faster, until we were on his heels.

" . . . a dream of mine since I was a boy," he was saying. "I've been working on my invention for years. All through college, every single day of my life."

"Have you tried it out?" I asked.

"Yes, and no," Dr. Wentmeyer said as we turned left and started down another long hallway.

"What do you mean by that?" Kara asked.

"I've only traveled to the not-so-distant past," he replied. "I haven't traveled more than a few years. But it works! That's what's important. Ah! Here we are."

He turned and pushed a steel door open. Kara and I followed, and Midnight trotted along behind.

The room was big. Once again, we were met with all kinds of junk piled high and scattered all over the place. There were shelves along the walls that were piled with things. Several tables, their surfaces stacked with junk, stood near the walls. And there were numerous metal folding chairs. Some of them were broken, some were folded and leaning against the wall. A few metal chairs sat tucked next to tables. It was amazing he was able to work with so much debris strewn about. On the wall was a huge, flat-screen television. The

49

monitor flashed pictures of various parts of the building inside and out, and I figured this was part of the security system.

And there was a powerful stench of smoke in the air, like burned plastic and hot metal.

In the middle of the room, however, was what looked to be an enormous shoe box—even taller than Dr. Wentmeyer. It had a door and what looked to be a single, huge window, but we couldn't see inside. All I could see were our reflections in the glass. There was a panel next to the door that had several rows of buttons. A couple of them were blinking yellow, green, and red.

"That's it?" I asked.

Dr. Wentmeyer beamed. "That's the Time Retranspositioning and Sub-Molecular Reducing Teleporter," he said.

I looked up and saw a dark, charred spot on the ceiling, nearly as big as the time machine itself.

"What happened up there?" I asked.

"Oh, just a little experimental mishap, I'm afraid," the doctor said. "Nothing to worry about."

*"That's* your time machine?" Kara asked. "How does it fly? I mean . . . there's no place for it to go. How does it leave the room?"

"That's what's so brilliant about my invention!" the doctor exclaimed. "You see, the machine travels on a molecular level. It changes into quadrillions of particles that are invisible to the naked eye. In fact, when the machine travels back in time, it will be invisible to anyone or anything. No one will be able to see it. However, anyone *inside* the machine will be able to see outside and watch what's going on."

My jaw fell. "You mean we could go back in time and watch the Declaration of Independence being signed, and no one would know we were watching?" I asked.

"Exactly!" Dr. Wentmeyer said.

"Or the Wright Brothers' plane fly at Kitty Hawk?" Kara asked.

"Yes!" Dr. Wentmeyer said. "It's all possible, thanks to my new machine. Would you like to try it out?"

"But what about your yard outside?" I asked. "And the windows?"

51

"You can do that when we return," the doctor said with a wave of his hand. "Besides: I'm excited to show someone my new invention. You'll be my first passengers!"

"I don't know," Kara said, shaking her head. "It looks dangerous." She looked worried.

"There's nothing dangerous about it at all," the doctor replied. "Look."

He strode to a table and picked up a digital camera. He turned it on and showed us the viewing screen. The image of a rocket of some sort appeared.

"What's that?" I asked.

"That's a picture of the first Apollo moon mission in 1969," he replied. "I took that picture fifteen minutes ago, when I traveled back in time to see it blast off!"

I was amazed and excited. *Time Travel?* I thought. *I never imagined it would be possible.*

"How long will we be gone?" I asked.

"When we travel into the past, there will be no time lost at all. We could spend hours in one location. When we return, only a few seconds will have passed."

"Can Midnight go?" I asked.

"I don't see why not," the doctor replied, and he walked to the large contraption. "It's perfectly safe," he said. He pressed a button, and the door automatically slid open. Then, he stepped inside and turned to face us.

"How about it?" he said with a grin. "Want to go for a ride?"

I *knew* I should've said no. I *knew* we should have turned, ran, and never looked back.

But traveling through time seemed so exciting, so incredible—and Kara and I would be the first kids to ever do it.

I looked at Kara. "I'll go if you go," I said.

Kara looked at Dr. Wentmeyer, then back to me. She shrugged.

"Well, it really *would* be cool to travel through time," she said."

Just then, Midnight barked. I don't know if he was barking to say 'yes,' or barking to say 'no.' But he was wagging his tail. It was as if he was excited, too.

"Okay," I said. "We'll do it."

However, we were about to find out that Dr.

Wentmeyer was wrong about one thing: time travel, as it turns out, is *far* from safe. In fact, time travel can be *deadly*.

And we were about to find out why.

# 9

"Ready?" Dr. Wentmeyer asked.

Only minutes before, we'd been standing in his laboratory. Dr. Wentmeyer found his shoe: it had been under one of his tables. How he lost it I don't know, and I didn't ask.

Now, we were seated inside his time machine. The interior was a bit crude, too, as it seemed the doctor had salvaged whatever he could to make his machine. The chairs we sat in were old seats removed from a car. They were worn and faded. The floor was metal, and it was stained and scuffed. On one wall, there was a tall panel filled with all sorts of dials, switches, blinking lights, and a computer keyboard with a screen above it.

Dr. Wentmeyer was busy fumbling with the dials and telling us how his invention worked. He used a lot of big, scientific words I'd never heard before, so I really didn't understand everything he was talking about. Kara was confused, too.

"But, if we travel back in time, will we be able to change things?" she asked. "And, if we do, won't that change things forever?"

She had a good point.

Dr. Wentmeyer shook his head.

"We will only travel as observers," the doctor replied. "We can only *watch* history; we cannot change it. Since we won't be able to be seen, we won't be a disruption."

Still, I was a little nervous. I wasn't sure how his machine worked, but I was sure any sort of time travel was dangerous. But Dr. Wentmeyer was confident we'd be fine.

"Just think," he said. "In the future, school field trips will involve traveling back and seeing important historical events. We'll be able to learn more than ever before by actually witnessing history in the making!"

The doctor turned to face us. His hair was still a messy fire of gray streaked with black soot, and grease remained on his arms, face, and shirt. Either he didn't know what he looked like, or he didn't care. Maybe a little of both.

"I think we're ready," he said. "Now: where would you like to travel in the past?"

I stared at him for a moment. So did Kara. The question seemed so crazy that it really didn't register. The doctor was actually asking us what historical event from the past we'd like to see!

"How far in the past can we go back?" Kara asked.

"As far as you wish," the doctor replied. "Remember: my invention isn't like a car or an airplane. The traveling we do can't be measured in miles. It would be just as easy to travel back one hundred years as it would to travel back one thousand."

*Holy crow,* I thought. *We're actually going to do this! We're actually going to travel back in time!*

"Well," I said, "in school last year, we learned all about Abraham Lincoln's Gettysburg address in 1863. Could we travel back to that?"

Dr. Wentmeyer's eyes lit up like spotlights. "An excellent idea!" he said, and he turned to the panel and began tapping on a computer keyboard.

"Gettysburg, Pennsylvania, in the year eighteen hundred and sixty three," he said as he typed. He paused and turned to me. "Tell me: do you happen to know the exact date and time?"

"November nineteenth," I said. "I'm not sure what time, but Lincoln's address was in the afternoon."

Dr. Wentmeyer turned and continued tapping on the keyboard.

All the while, Midnight remained at my feet. He'd become bored quickly, and I think he was napping.

"Ready?" the doctor asked as he took a seat.

Kara gave me a nervous glance. Maybe she was a little scared. I know I was.

"Ready," I said.

"Don't we need some sort of seat belt?" Kara asked.

Dr. Wentmeyer shook his head, and his hair wiggled. He looked funny, like some mad scientist from the movies. I nearly laughed out loud.

"No," he replied. "Remember: we aren't traveling in *distance*. We are traveling through *time*."

Just then, Midnight got up and stretched. He wagged his tail, walked to Dr. Wentmeyer, and sniffed his knee.

"And you, Mr. Doggie," the doctor said, "will be the very first hound to travel time. How do you like that?"

He reached down and patted Midnight's head, but when he drew his arm back, his elbow bumped some of the switches and dials on the wall behind him. There was a sudden, loud buzzing of electricity, like an enormous engine was revving up.

Dr. Wentmeyer spun.

Then, he gasped. His arms and hands whirred as he flicked switches and dials. He frantically typed at the computer keyboard.

*"No, no, no!"* he shouted. *"No! This cannot happen! Children! Hurry! We must get out now!"*

And that's when the panel erupted in a shower of sparks . . . and everything went black.

**10**

The noise continued to grow and the floor began to vibrate, causing my chair to tremble. Midnight let out a yelp and surprised me—I couldn't see him—by jumping into my lap. The panel of blinking lights on the wall had gone dark, and the inside of the time machine was like being in a cave.

*"What happened?!?!"* Kara screeched.

*"There's been a terrible malfunction!"* Dr. Wentmeyer said from somewhere in the darkness. *"I can't get the door open . . . I can't stop the*

*machine!"*

The vibration beneath my feet continued to grow stronger. My chair shook violently, and it felt like I was moving. Midnight remained in my lap, whimpering softly. I felt bad for him: he was just as afraid as I was.

A thin strip of light appeared, and I recognized it as a small flashlight beam. It wasn't very bright, but I could see the dim splash of light illuminate a portion of the panel. Dr. Wentmeyer worked furiously.

Meanwhile, the contraption around us continued to rock, and the loud humming droned on. It sounded like we were sitting right next to a jet engine.

I pulled Midnight close and held him tight. He wasn't whimpering anymore, but I could tell he was still scared. He didn't like loud noises, and the raging hum was freaking him out.

"Ah! I think I've got it!" Dr. Wentmeyer said. His voice sounded hopeful.

The roaring hum began to fade. The shaking lessened.

In the darkness, I heard Kara's voice. She

sounded scared, too. "Are . . . are we . . . are we going to be all right?"

"Yes, yes," the doctor said. "Just a minor problem, I think. Not as bad as I thought."

The humming subsided and became a steady, low drone. The rocking of the machine stopped.

"Yes, we'll be fine," the doctor repeated.

"What happened?" I asked.

"It's what's called 'overshooting the runway,'" Dr. Wentmeyer replied. "When I bumped the controls, it caused the machine to malfunction. I don't think it's anything to worry about. We just traveled a little farther back than 1863."

"How far back?" Kara asked. "Am I going to be home for lunch?"

"Certainly, certainly," the doctor said. "I'm not sure how far back we—"

Suddenly, a bright light filled the window opposite Dr. Wentmeyer. Since we'd been in total darkness, my eyes weren't ready for it. I raised my hands to block the bright light.

I squinted, straining to see. As my eyes

adjusted, I could see the ground outside . . . which was strange. After all: we were in the time machine that was in Dr. Wentmeyer's laboratory. I shouldn't be able to see dirt.

*Unless,* I thought, *we actually traveled somewhere back in time.*

A low rumble began in Midnight's throat. The rumble became a growl, and then he barked.

I lowered my hands. Still squinting, I strained to see out the window.

Something moved.

Something *big.*

At first, I thought it was a horse. But as my eyes adjusted to the light, I realized what I was seeing wasn't a horse or any sort of farm animal.

*I was staring at a living dinosaur!*

When Dr. Wentmeyer said we overshot the runway, he wasn't kidding. We overshot it by a few million years!

*"What is that?!?!"* Kara shrieked as she stared out the window. I thought her eyes were going to fall out of her head!

Dr. Wentmeyer was still working at the control panel and tapping at the computer keyboard. He turned.

"My goodness!" he said excitedly. "It's a dinosaur!" He seemed pleased, and not at all concerned about the creature that couldn't have been more than a dozen yards from us.

*This is crazy,* I thought. I guess part of me didn't actually believe Dr. Wentmeyer's contraption would actually *work.* Well, it worked, all right. Maybe it worked *too* well.

Midnight was still growling, and he leapt from my lap and approached the window. His tail stood straight and stiff, and the hair on his back stood up in a ridge.

"Can . . . can that thing see us?" I asked.

Dr. Wentmeyer shook his head. "We are completely invisible," he said. "Although we can see him, he can't see us."

Still, I was scared. The dinosaur we were watching must've been twenty feet tall! I had no idea what kind he was, as I'd never seen one like it in any of the books I'd read. His skin was a dirty, reddish-brown color. He stood on his hind legs, and his tail was nearly as long as his body. His arms were very long, and we watched as he used them to reach up and bend a tree branch. The creature pulled the branch to his mouth, and he chewed at the leaves, which were long and thick, like palm leaves.

"There's another one!" Kara said, pointing. "Way over there!"

In the distance, I saw the dinosaur Kara was pointing at. It appeared to be the same kind as the one that was close to us.

"Absolutely fantastic!" Dr. Wentmeyer said. "My Time Retranspositioning and Sub-Molecular Reducing Teleporter is a complete and total success!"

Midnight was still standing with his nose at the window, looking out and growling softly.

"Midnight," I said, "it's okay."

He looked at me and wagged his tail once, then returned his attention to the dinosaur that was chewing the leaves.

"Incredible!" Dr. Wentmeyer said. "Do you see? Do you see why my invention will be the most important discovery in the history of man?"

"It sure is cool," I said.

The dinosaur stopped chewing and turned his head quickly. His attention seemed to be diverted by something we couldn't see. Then, it took off running. His claw-like feet thundered on the ground, kicking up dust and dirt. In seconds, he was gone.

"Strange," Dr. Wentmeyer said. "Something must've scared him away."

In the distance, we saw the other dinosaur doing the same thing: running away. Soon, he, too, had vanished in a forest thick with trees that had huge, paw-like green leaves.

"I wonder what they're afraid of," Kara said.

Midnight's growling became louder. I'd never heard him sound so fierce. He bared his teeth and snarled, and his nose was pressing against the glass.

"What is it, boy?" I asked.

Something dark raced by the window. It wasn't very big—maybe twice the size of Midnight—but it moved so fast I didn't get a good look at it. Then, another one whizzed by. And another.

Then, one ran right in front of the window—and stopped. It was a dinosaur, for sure. He had long legs and a long tail, and his head came up to my chest. His skin was leathery and dark gray. His arms were short. His mouth was open, exposing rows upon rows of ferociously sharp teeth.

Midnight was growling so viciously that he was foaming at the mouth.

"It's okay, buddy," I said. "He can't see us."

The dinosaur took a step closer. He cocked his head to the side, as if—

*As if he was looking at us.*

He took another step closer.

Midnight continued to growl. Then, he began snapping at the window.

The dinosaur stepped closer. His head bobbed and ducked in short, jerky movements. He was only a few inches from the window.

I turned to Dr. Wentmeyer. "Are you sure he can't—"

*Suddenly, the dinosaur lunged at the glass! He was trying to attack Midnight!*

The dinosaur hit the window with such force that I thought the glass would shatter. I raised my arms to cover my face, just in case.

Thankfully, the window remained intact. The dinosaur hit the glass with his snout, then began snapping at the window with his teeth and clawing at it with his front paws.

Meanwhile, Midnight was in full attack mode. He was standing inches from the glass, growling and snarling at the dinosaur. But, I knew he'd be no match for the brutal creature on the other side of the glass. If the window shattered, the dinosaur would most certainly tear my dog to shreds.

Of course, the creature would probably do the same to us, too!

"I thought you said we were invisible!" I shouted as the dinosaur snapped at the glass.

Dr. Wentmeyer looked shocked. "We are!" he said. He turned to the panel and began typing something into the computer keyboard. "At least, I *thought* we were!"

"Well, that dinosaur can see Midnight!" I said. "He can probably see us, too!"

Dr. Wentmeyer tapped furiously at the keyboard. "I don't understand," he muttered. "It should be working, unless it was somehow damaged during our travel."

*"Midnight!"* I shouted. *"Here!"*

Midnight looked at me, then at the dinosaur. He backed away, but his attention was still focused on the creature.

"Good boy," I said, and I reached out and grabbed his collar. "Sit."

The dinosaur backed away, but he was still

watching. He looked like he was ready to attack again at any moment.

"I hope that window holds," Kara said.

Dr. Wentmeyer spoke while he typed. "The glass is another invention of mine. It is impossible to break. It's made of a mixture of glass and plastic."

*It's too bad he didn't use the glass for the windows at his house,* I thought. *Then, the window wouldn't have broken when the softball hit it. We wouldn't be in the mess we were.*

After a few minutes, the dinosaur darted away. There were no other creatures to see.

"I can't believe we were attacked by a real dinosaur!" Kara said.

"This is almost like what happened in Detroit, Michigan," I said. "When those T-Rexs invaded the city." A few years ago, a crazy thing happened: a couple of dinosaurs appeared out of nowhere and nearly destroyed the city of Detroit and the surrounding areas. They disappeared without a trace, and no one knew how or why. Some guy even wrote a book about it.

"It's a good thing there aren't dinosaurs like

that in West Virginia," Kara said. "They'd cause all kinds of trouble. There's no way Midnight would be able to fend off a creature like that. Did you see his teeth?"

"Yeah," I said, patting Midnight's head. "But you sure are a brave dog." Midnight thumped his tail on the floor.

Dr. Wentmeyer stopped tapping at the computer keyboard. He looked grim.

"I have good news, and I have bad news," he said.

My head suddenly felt heavy, and my heart was a bowling ball in my chest.

"The good news is we can leave shortly," he continued.

That, of course, *was* good news.

But when he told us the bad news, I knew that a bad day was about to get a whole lot worse.

There was a long silence.

"What's the bad news?" Kara finally asked.

Dr. Wentmeyer heaved a sigh. He took his glasses off and rubbed his eyes. "We aren't invisible," he said. "We need to make a repair to the outside of the time machine. However, I must remain here to work on the computer while the repair is being made, so I can shout instructions and type in coordinates." He put his glasses back on and looked at Kara, then me. His face was serious, intense. "One of you will have to go outside and make the repair."

"You . . . you mean *out there?*" I said as I pointed outside. "Where the dinosaurs are?"

Dr. Wentmeyer nodded. "I'm afraid it's the only way. Somehow, the photomallification transponding receiver has been repositioned. It's a simple adjustment, really. But once it's fixed, the time machine will be invisible again, and we'll be able to leave."

I looked at Kara, and she looked at me. She didn't say anything, but her eyes told me everything I needed to know.

*I'll do it if I have to,* she was thinking, *but I'd really rather have you do it, Brandon.*

"How long is it going to take?" I asked.

"Only a few minutes," the doctor replied. "The photomallification transponding receiver is at the front of the time machine. There is a dial that needs to be adjusted to its proper place. All you'll need to do is follow my directions that I'll shout to you."

"But what about *them?*" I asked. "What if those things attack? There's no way I'll be able to fight them off. You saw how vicious they are. One of them tried to attack Midnight through the glass."

"I didn't say it wouldn't be dangerous," Dr. Wentmeyer said. "That's a risk we have to take, if we want to return to our home in the future."

*Terrific,* I thought. *How am I going to explain this to Mom? 'Sorry, Mom . . . I was stuck millions of years in the past because Dr. Wentmeyer's contraption broke, and we were attacked by dinosaurs. That's why I'm late for lunch.'*

She wouldn't believe me for half a second.

"Well, if it's the only way," I said, "I guess we don't have a choice. Tell me what I have to do."

Dr. Wentmeyer explained everything to me. Sure, it *sounded* easy enough . . . but I was more worried about being attacked by a dinosaur. So far, however, we hadn't seen any more around. Maybe they had left the area.

When Dr. Wentmeyer was done explaining, I stood.

"Let's get this over with," I said, "so we can go home. Traveling through time is cool, but I'm not too hip about being attacked by real

77

dinosaurs."

"Be careful," Kara said.

Midnight stood and looked at me hopefully. He wagged his tail. "No, buddy, you can't come. Not this time. I'll be right back."

"Ready?" Dr. Wentmeyer asked.

"No," I replied. "But that doesn't matter."

I really didn't want to go outside where we'd seen those dinosaurs, but I really didn't have any other choice.

The doctor tapped at the keyboard, then flicked a couple of switches. The door panel slid to the right, and hot, tropical air drifted inside. It was thick and heavy.

I looked around. I could see large rocks and boulders and towering trees with enormous leaves.

No dinosaurs.

I leaned out the door and continued looking around. It was so strange. The surroundings looked nothing like I'd seen anywhere.

"I don't see any dinosaurs," I said and took a step outside, a step back in time, millions of years.

To my great relief, I still didn't see any

dinosaurs. In fact, I saw no life at all, other than the trees. There were no prehistoric birds in the sky, and I didn't see or hear any insects buzzing about.

*This won't be so bad,* I thought, not knowing I was being watched at that very moment.

# 14

Finding the photomallification transponding receiver was easy enough. Dr. Wentmeyer had explained it was something to help create a shield of invisibility around the time machine. While I didn't completely understand how it worked, I knew it had to be fixed before we could leave.

"Do you see it?" the doctor shouted from inside the machine.

"Yeah," I shouted back.

"Turn the dial to the right, until I tell you to stop."

The dial he was talking about was the size of a dinner plate. It turned easily in my hand.

"Keep turning," Dr. Wentmeyer said. "You're doing fine."

As I continued to turn the knob, a strange thing happened: the time machine began to vanish!

"Hey!" I shouted. "The time machine is disappearing!"

"That's what's supposed to happen," Dr. Wentmeyer said. "Soon, you won't be able to see the door to get back in. Kara, put your arm through the door. Brandon won't be able to see the time machine, but he'll see your arm and know where the door is."

I glanced behind me. The time machine was now almost completely invisible. Suddenly, Kara's arm appeared out of nowhere! It was very strange. All I could see was a portion of her arm from her elbow to her hand. It looked like a severed arm, suspended in midair!

"Turn the dial just a little bit more," Dr. Wentmeyer called out.

I continued to turn the knob while I looked

around at the strange surroundings. It was still hard to believe I was looking millions of years into the past.

Not far off, I heard a soft rustling. A few branches and leaves fluttered near the ground, like something had moved them. I stared, my alarm growing.

Then, I saw a pair of eyes in the shadows of the leaves.

And a claw.

It was one of *them*.

"Perfect!" Dr. Wentmeyer exclaimed. "It's fixed!"

But it was too late. I turned to race back to the door . . . but the dinosaur had already made the first move and was racing toward me!

The time machine was now completely invisible;
I could see right through it. I couldn't see the
doctor, or Kara, or Midnight. However, I knew
where the door was because I could see Kara's
arm—and only her arm—protruding out. It was
really strange to see, but I was getting used to
seeing strange things.

I turned and sprang toward Kara's arm, not
even taking the time to see how far away the
dinosaur was. I knew he was fast, but I was hoping
I was faster.

In three long strides, I reached Kara's arm. I grasped her hand at the exact same moment the dinosaur caught my pant leg.

*"Pull, Kara, pull!"* I screeched.

She did, and I tumbled inside the time machine. Which was really weird, because now that I was inside, I could see everything clearly. I could see the floor, the walls, Kara, and Dr. Wentmeyer.

The door began to close, and I yanked my pant leg out of the dinosaur's mouth. I heard the sound of tearing cloth as I pulled my leg away . . . and just in time, too. The door was closing quickly. I barely had enough time to get my foot inside before the door closed on it.

I laid on the floor, gasping for breath. *" Holy crow!"* I said. *"That was too close! That thing nearly got me!"*

The dinosaur appeared at the window, and Midnight stood, letting out a low, deep rumble.

"Shhh, Midnight," I said.

"The dinosaur is confused," Dr. Wentmeyer said. "He knows something is here, but he can't see it, now that we're invisible."

"I wonder what kind of dinosaur it is," Kara said.

"According to the computer, we've traveled back in time eighty-three millions years," the doctor replied. "We are in what is commonly referred to as the Cretaceous period. Judging by the size of the dinosaur, and his swift movements, I would guess it is probably a velociraptor."

"Wow!" I said. I'd heard about velociraptors before, and I saw drawings of them in books. But the ones we saw were smaller than what I thought they would be.

"See his sharp, curved claws?" Dr. Wentmeyer said. "The velociraptor is a meat-eating predator dinosaur. Although he is smaller than most dinosaurs, it's been thought the velociraptor was one of the most vicious dinosaurs ever to exist. They also had a very large brain, making them one of the most intelligent dinosaurs ever to exist."

Midnight was still growling softly as the dinosaur moved along the window.

"Can he see us?" Kara asked.

"Not anymore," the doctor replied. "Now

that the photomallification transponding receiver is fixed. Oh, he knows we're here, all right. He can feel the side of the time machine. But he can no longer see us."

Now that I was safely inside the time machine, I was fascinated with the dinosaur. Here we were, eighty-three million years in the past, and I was only a few feet away from one of the most ferocious dinosaurs ever to walk the planet!

While we watched, another velociraptor appeared. And another. They approached the window, and they, too, seemed curious. One of them bumped into the time machine because he couldn't see it. They scratched at the glass with their claws and cocked their heads to the side in jerky, quick movements.

"They move like giant chickens," Kara said.

"This is all very fascinating," Dr. Wentmeyer said, "but we need to be on our way. I have some adjustments I'd like to make, but I don't dare make them until we have safely returned to the future and my laboratory."

"I can't wait to tell my friends!" Kara said.

Dr. Wentmeyer shook his head. "You

mustn't say anything to anyone until I have my invention perfected," he said. "It's going to take a couple of weeks. I'm going to have to work on the photomallification transponding receiver to make sure we don't have another mishap. Then, the world will be ready to know, and you can tell everyone about what you saw today." He looked at me. "Agreed?"

I shrugged. "Sure," I said. "Nobody would believe us, anyway."

"Soon, they will," Dr. Wentmeyer said. He turned and made some adjustments to the panel, then began tapping into the keyboard.

"There's another one," Kara said, pointing at the window. Beyond, in the distance, another velociraptor was approaching.

"I think I read somewhere that velociraptors hunt in packs, like wolves," I said.

"As long as they aren't hunting us," Kara said, "they can hunt any way they want."

The time machine gave off a loud hum.

"Sorry to cut our adventure short," Dr. Wentmeyer said, "but it's time to leave. I have work to finish, and you two have a lot of cleaning up to do around my laboratory."

*Rats,* I thought. I was hoping he'd forget about that.

The hum grew louder, and the velociraptors stepped back. Still, they looked curious. Dr. Wentmeyer was sure they couldn't see us, but I wasn't so certain.

The window blurred and went gray. The humming grew louder still, and soon, we could no longer see through the window.

"Here we go," Dr. Wentmeyer said. "Hang on."

The humming grew louder still. But then, we heard another sound: several loud thumps above us.

We looked up.

"What was that?" I asked.

"I'm sure it was nothing," Dr. Wentmeyer said.

Oh, it was *something,* all right. We didn't know it at the time, but we were returning to the future . . . with some uninvited guests.

The time machine began to vibrate and shake. Midnight had been standing, facing the window. Now, he sat at my feet.

"We're on our way!" Dr. Wentmeyer exclaimed.

The machine shook and rocked. I was amazed that time travel was actually so easy. Dr. Wentmeyer was right: his invention would be one of the most important discoveries in human history . . . and Kara and I had been a part of it! Maybe Dr. Wentmeyer would let us take another trip with him somewhere.

I looked down at my pant leg. The cloth was torn neatly, and a few shreds dangled. I hated to think what would have happened if that velociraptor had taken hold of my foot!

*And how am I going to explain this to Mom?* I wondered. *How am I going to tell her that a dinosaur tore my pants? She'll think I lost my mind.*

Dr. Wentmeyer was still seated in front of the panel, typing into the keyboard.

"Almost there," he said.

The quaking and shaking slowed, and the humming became softer. The doctor flicked a couple of switches, turned a few dials, then turned to us.

"We're home!" he said, clasping his hands together. "Now . . . what do you think of my invention?"

"I think it's awesome!" I said.

"Me, too!" Kara said. "I hope we get to do it again sometime."

"Oh, perhaps," Dr. Wentmeyer said. "We'll see."

He turned to the panel and pressed a

button. The door slid open with a *whoosh,* revealing the inside of his messy laboratory.

"It's like we never left," Kara said.

"In all actuality," Dr. Wentmeyer said, "we didn't. It's very complicated. We didn't really move anywhere, we sort of 'shifted.'"

I knew I'd probably never understand exactly how time travel works, but Dr. Wentmeyer sure did. He'd spent his life working on it . . . and he'd figured it out. He was going to be famous, and I knew it would be only a matter of time before we saw him on television. Kara and I might even be on television, too, telling people all about our trip eighty-three million years into the past!

I stood, and so did Kara. I was about to step out of the machine and into the laboratory when Midnight began to growl. He was looking up at the ceiling.

"Hush, Midnight," I said.

But he didn't listen to me.

*That's strange,* I thought. *He always obeys me. He always does what I tell him to do.*

"Midnight," I said sternly. "Quiet."

Midnight didn't listen. Instead, he growled

93

louder and bared his teeth.

I looked up at the ceiling, and so did Kara. Even Dr. Wentmeyer looked up.

From above, we heard a scraping noise. It sounded like something was on top of the time machine.

"Odd," Dr. Wentmeyer said. "The machine is shut down. I wonder what could be making that noise?"

Dr. Wentmeyer's answer came in a flurry of loud scrapes and scratches. Then, there was a crash somewhere in the laboratory. We heard another noise above us and yet another crash in the room.

And then, in the doorway, the past met the present. Eighty-three million years ago, velociraptors roamed the earth.

Eighty-three million years later, one was standing in Dr. Wentmeyer's laboratory!

# 17

We stared in horror as the velociraptor glared at us. Midnight's growling reached a feverous pitch, and I grabbed his collar before he could attack the dinosaur. I don't think he understood there was no way he would win a fight with a velociraptor.

The dinosaur gazed at us curiously, like he was seeing something new and strange. Of course, he'd never seen a human being before . . . and he probably wondered what we would taste like!

Quickly, Dr. Wentmeyer spun and flicked a switch on the panel. The door slid closed just as the creature attacked. We could hear him pawing and scratching on the other side.

"This is a disaster!" Dr. Wentmeyer said. "We should not have brought something from the past into the future! It's breaking all laws of time travel!"

We heard more scratching from above. At least two velociraptors had hitched a ride on the time machine . . . maybe more.

"Is there any way we can see out the window?" I asked.

Dr. Wentmeyer tapped at the computer keyboard. The window, which had been black, turned a fuzzy gray. Then it was clear, and we could see into the laboratory.

The velociraptor had moved away from the time machine and was stalking about the room. He took a bite of a table leg, causing the whole thing to crash to the ground.

"This is horrible!" the doctor said. "I never thought something like this could happen!"

"What do we do now?" Kara asked.

"We must find a way to get them home," Dr. Wentmeyer said.

"Are you crazy?!?!" I said. "I'm not going anywhere near those things!"

Another velociraptor leapt from the top of the time machine and landed on the floor. Then another.

"There are three of them," Dr. Wentmeyer said. "This is awful. This shouldn't have happened."

"Hey, let's just be glad we're in here and they're out there," I said.

"But if they somehow get out of my laboratory and outside, the world could be in for a lot of trouble," Dr. Wentmeyer said.

"Don't you have a fence all around your property?" Kara asked.

The doctor nodded. "Yes, the fence goes all around the property. But the velociraptors might be able to tear through it . . . especially if they see something on the other side they really want."

While we watched, the three velociraptors searched the laboratory. They looked keenly interested as they walked about, making strange grunting and screeching noises.

Finally, one of them vanished through the

97

open door. The two others followed.

"We must do something," Dr. Wentmeyer said.

"Like what?" I asked. "Those things will tear us to shreds!"

"This is my fault," the doctor said. "I'll do whatever I can to undo what I have done."

He flicked a lever on the panel, and the time machine door opened.

"You two stay here," he said. "Whatever happens, don't come out."

And before I had time to ask him what he was going to do, he had already hurried out the door, where he pressed a button on the time machine. The door closed.

"He's crazy!" Kara said. "Those dinosaurs will eat him up!"

From inside the time machine, we watched Dr. Wentmeyer rummaging through the laboratory. After a moment, he found something that looked like a tennis racquet. In fact, that's what it was—except it had a bigger handle and all sorts of wires wrapped around it. There were also some small, silver boxes attached to it. It looked like it might be one of his inventions.

"That's not going to stop one of those velociraptors," Kara said.

"We're about to find out," I said, pointing to the laboratory door. "One is coming back into the room, right now!"

# 18

Thankfully, Dr. Wentmeyer saw the dinosaur at the same time we did. How he was going to defend himself, I had no idea. The thing that he'd picked up certainly didn't look like a weapon. Maybe he could swat at flies with it, but I doubted he'd be able to fight off a velociraptor!

Midnight started to growl again, and I patted his head. "Take it easy, buddy," I said. He wagged his tail and looked at me, but he continued growling softly.

Dr. Wentmeyer was holding out the tennis

racquet like it was a sword. He sure looked funny, with his messy, soot-filled gray hair and his tattered and stained white shirt! He looked like he'd already been in one battle and was preparing for another. Sure, the doctor was tall, and the velociraptor was only about half his size . . . but it was easy to see that the dinosaur had the upper hand when it came to hunting prey.

The dinosaur spotted Dr. Wentmeyer and stopped moving. He cocked his head to the side, sizing up his prey.

*"I sure hope Dr. Wentmeyer knows what he's doing,"* Kara whispered. *"Otherwise, that thing is going to rip him apart."*

The velociraptor took a cautious step, slow and catlike. Dr. Wentmeyer didn't move.

At my side, Midnight continued to growl softly.

The velociraptor took another step forward. His mouth was open slightly, and we could see his teeth, sharp and dangerous.

Still, Dr. Wentmeyer didn't move. He held out the strange, tennis racquet-thing, as if it was all the protection he needed.

The velociraptor was now only about ten feet from the doctor. He bobbed his head from side to side and sniffed the air. All the while, his eyes never left Dr. Wentmeyer. Last summer, I watched a hawk in a tree. The bird was scanning the ground, until he suddenly saw something. I watched the bird watching whatever was on the ground, and I could even see him tense up. Finally, the hawk dropped from the branch and shot straight to the ground. Seconds later, he flew away with a mouse.

That's what the velociraptor seemed to be doing: waiting for the perfect moment to strike. He'd hunted for food all his life, and I'm sure he was good at it. He'd have to be, if he wanted to survive.

The velociraptor crouched even lower to the ground.

"The way he's crouching like that, he looks like he's trying to hide," Kara said.

"I don't know what he's trying to do," I replied. "It's almost like he's—"

The velociraptor suddenly sprang into the air. He didn't run; He didn't need to. He used his powerful hind legs to leap into the air with lightning speed.

There was no way Dr. Wentmeyer could be prepared. Even if he had a gun or some other weapon, he wouldn't be able to fend off something that fast, that strong. We could only watch as a flurry of razor sharp claws and teeth sailed through the air, straight for their prey:

*Dr. Wentmeyer.*

The speed of the velociraptor was incredible. In one calculated, powerful leap, he attacked Dr. Wentmeyer.

Dr. Wentmeyer, however, stood his ground, still holding the odd-looking racquet-thing in front of him.

And an amazing thing happened.

Not only did the attacking dinosaur miss his prey, he fell to the ground, limp and lifeless! Dr. Wentmeyer had backed out of the creature's way and he sailed past him, falling to the floor, unmoving. The tennis-racquet-thing never even touched the creature!

Dr. Wentmeyer remained a few feet away. He held the racquet out, prepared to defend himself again if necessary.

"What is that thing he's holding?" I wondered out loud.

"Whatever it is, it killed the dinosaur," Kara said. "It must be really powerful."

Dr. Wentmeyer took a step toward the dinosaur. Satisfied that the velociraptor wasn't going to attack again, he turned and raced for the laboratory door, slamming it closed and bolting the lock. Then, he hurried over to the time machine, tapped at the panel, and the door opened.

"Quickly!" he said. "You must help me. We've got to contain the dinosaur!"

"Midnight!" I said. "Stay!" Midnight sat as Kara and I stepped out of the time machine. "What is that thing that you used on the velociraptor?" I asked.

Dr. Wentmeyer held up the gadget. It was, as I suspected, a tennis racquet. However, it had been modified with lots of small metal things. There were no strings: just a few copper wires that criss-crossed.

"This is an invention I made years ago," Dr. Wentmeyer explained. "It's an electronic brain wave inhibitor."

"A *what?*" Kara asked.

"What it does is stop all brain waves. When that dinosaur attacked, I activated the unit. When he got close, the electromagnetic activity in the racquet made him cease all brain activity. It caused him to fall asleep."

"So, he's not dead?" I asked.

Dr. Wentmeyer shook his head. "Not at all. He's only unconscious for just a few minutes. He'll wake up very soon, so we must hurry."

"What are we going to do with him?" I asked.

"I have a steel box in the corner that should be big enough and strong enough," he said. "Actually, it's a smaller, experimental version of my time machine that didn't work. It's over there."

He pointed, but the only things I saw were piles of junk. Maybe there was a steel box in the corner, but it was buried beneath broken appliances.

The doctor made his way around tables piled with junk. He pulled away a few items—an electric mixer; several toasters; two fans; a thick, black blanket, and a leaf blower that had wires hanging out. It seemed incredible that he used all these things—ordinary household items—to create so many different inventions . . . including a time machine.

"Here it is," he said. "Help me clear away this stuff."

I sidestepped around the motionless velociraptor. His mouth was open, and his tongue hung out. Again, I could see how long and sharp his teeth were. I shuddered to think that one had actually come close enough to tear my pant leg.

Kara and I helped the doctor clear the debris away. Beneath everything was a silver-gray box made of steel. It was as big as a washing machine. While we watched, Dr. Wentmeyer bent over and flipped a lever. One of the sides of the box opened. There was nothing inside, except for a panel of switches and dials similar to what was in the big time machine from which we'd emerged from.

"This should be big and strong enough to hold him," the doctor said. "Come. Help me drag the dinosaur over here."

"Ewww!" Kara said. "You mean we have to *touch* the thing?!?!"

"It's won't be any different than touching a lizard or a snake," Dr. Wentmeyer assured her.

"I don't like touching them, either," she said.

We walked to the velociraptor. He was still motionless, but I could see the gentle rising and falling of his ribs as he breathed.

"We might just be able to drag him over," the doctor said. He reached down and grabbed the velociraptor's front legs. "Amazing," he said, looking at the dinosaur's claws. "We're getting a close-up look at a creature that's been extinct for over eighty-million years!"

I grabbed the creature's hind legs. Dr. Wentmeyer was right: the dinosaur's skin felt like the skin of a lizard. It was warm and leathery and rough.

"Pull," the doctor ordered. I did as he said and was surprised to find the dinosaur lighter than

I expected. I don't think we could have lifted him off the floor, but we had no problem dragging him across the tile.

Kara stood nearby with her hands on her hips. There was no way she was going to touch the thing.

We pushed the dinosaur into the metal box without any difficulty. Actually, the box was plenty big enough. The velociraptor would have enough room to move around inside when he woke up.

The problem was this: before Dr. Wentmeyer could close the door, the dinosaur woke up in a fit and flurry of gnashing teeth and flailing claws!

If it hadn't been for quick thinking on the part of Dr. Wentmeyer, I don't know what might have happened. Just as the dinosaur woke up, the doctor jerked his hand away—and just in time, too. The velociraptor lunged forward, mouth open, teeth exposed, and Dr. Wentmeyer quickly slammed the door shut and turned the bolt. There was a dull, loud click as the lock secured the door.

Inside the steel box, the velociraptor was furious. He made screeching and wailing sounds as he scratched with his claws and teeth, trying to get out. Midnight, still sitting in the time machine, heard the commotion. He started barking and growling.

"It's okay, boy," I said. Midnight stopped barking, but he continued to growl softly.

Dr. Wentmeyer spoke. "The dinosaur won't be able to get out of the box," he said. "Now, we have to locate the other two."

"I'm not going out there," I said.

Kara shook her head, and her blond hair slapped her face. "Me, neither," she said.

"We won't have to," the doctor said, pointing to the television monitor mounted on the wall. "I have security cameras placed all over the building, even outside. We should be able to find out where the other two are."

"Shouldn't we call the police or something?" I said. "Maybe they could help."

Dr. Wentmeyer shook his head. "I no longer have any phones," he said. "Too much of a distraction. People I don't even know call me all the time, trying to sell me things I don't need. I got rid of all my phones months ago."

I could see his point, but that also meant

something else. Kara and I couldn't call our parents and let them know what was going on. If we were stuck here for a long time, we'd have no way to contact them. Or anyone else, for that matter.

The velociraptor in the steel box was still clawing and scratching, screeching and screaming. Clearly, he didn't like being held captive.

Dr. Wentmeyer shifted a pile of papers on one of his desks. A number of papers tipped over and fell to the floor, but he paid them no mind. Besides: there were already papers scattered all over the place. A few more were hardly noticeable.

"Ah," he said. "Here we are. This is another invention of mine: a remote control that not only works the television, but also my time machine." He snapped up the remote control unit and pressed a button. Above, on the wall, the television monitor came on. At first, images were fuzzy and out of focus. Then, I could make out what appeared to be a room, similar to the room we were in. Dr. Wentmeyer pressed another button, and the image changed. Now, we saw a hallway . . . and a velociraptor! He was stalking down the hall, turning his head from side to side. His long tail dragged on the floor, swishing back and forth.

"There's one of them," the doctor said. "If we can keep them contained within the building, we might be able to capture them. Then, we can send them back to their own time with my machine."

I had no idea how he planned to do this. Not only did it sound dangerous . . . it sounded impossible. Sure, we'd been able to get one of them locked in a box, but what about the other two?

We watched the velociraptor walk along the hall. He would take a couple of steps, then look to the left, then to the right.

Then, he stopped at a window. He sniffed the air and looked around. His head made jerky movements from side to side.

Then, he crouched down.

*"No,"* Dr. Wentmeyer said. Alarm weighed heavily in his voice. *"If he gets outside, it might be impossible to capture him."*

Suddenly, Dr. Wentmeyer's hopes were

dashed as the velociraptor leapt, crashing through the window in a shattering shower of glass.

*He was outside!*

The dinosaur in the steel box continued to screech and claw and try to get out. He sure sounded mad!

However, our eyes were glued to the television monitor on the wall. The velociraptor we had been watching was gone. There were shards of glass on the tile floor.

"We've got to think quickly!" Dr. Wentmeyer said. "We have to stop those things!"

"Why don't you use that tennis-racquet-thingy to stop the other two?" Kara asked.

"I could," the doctor replied, "if I could fight

them one at a time. With two of them on the prowl, it might be too risky. One of them might attack while I was fending off the other one."

Dr. Wentmeyer pointed the remote control at the television and changed the channel. The monitor showed different rooms and hallways, but there was no sign of the one dinosaur that was still in the building—if, in fact, he was inside. We knew one was outside . . . but where was the other one?

"Let's look outside," the doctor said. He changed the channel again, and the television monitor switched to one of the outdoor cameras. We saw his black car and our bicycles.

No velociraptor.

He changed the channel again. "This is the north side of the building," Dr. Wentmeyer said. We saw a large field, and, in the distance, the tall fence.

No dinosaur.

"Let's try another angle," the doctor said, changing the channel again. The picture on the television monitor changed again . . . and this time, he found what he was looking for.

"There he is!" Dr. Wentmeyer said. "He's by

the southwest corner of the building!"

The velociraptor was hard to see, because the camera was so far away. But there was no mistaking what we were looking at. The dinosaur was walking warily, slowly, cocking his head from side to side, looking curiously at his surroundings. I had to wonder what he was thinking: only a few minutes ago, he had been with his buddies in his own world, eighty-three million years in the past. Here, in West Virginia, he was in completely different surroundings. The ground was different, the trees were different . . . even the air was different.

"So far, so good," Dr. Wentmeyer said. "As long as he doesn't try to get out through the fence or the gate."

"Do you think he's strong enough to break through the fence?" I asked.

Dr. Wentmeyer shook his head. "I don't think so," he said. "I think the fence is too high for him to jump over. And I don't think he'll be able to chew through the fence. His teeth are sharp, but they're not *that* sharp. My main concern now is finding out where the other dinosaur is. He's got to be here in the building, somewhere."

Dr. Wentmeyer was about to get his answer, and it didn't come from the television monitor. It came when there was a sudden, explosive shattering sound behind us!

The three of us turned, surprised by the sudden, loud noise.

"He's trying to get through the door!" Dr. Wentmeyer shouted. "Get into the time machine! You'll be safe in there! Hurry!"

Kara and I ran to the time machine and bounded through the open door. Midnight stood as we entered, wagging his tail.

There was another loud thump at the door that shook the entire laboratory. Meanwhile, the velociraptor trapped in the steel box continued scratching and clawing, trying to get out.

Dr. Wentmeyer punched a button on the outside panel of the time machine, and the door whisked closed. We were safely inside. Through the large window, we watched him pick up his electronic brain wave inhibitor and walk to the laboratory door. He stood there, waiting for the dinosaur to break through.

"Do you think the velociraptor is strong enough to break down the door?" Kara asked.

"I don't know," I said. "I hope not. But at least Dr. Wentmeyer is prepared with his electronic whatchamacallit."

Even from inside the time machine, we could hear the velociraptor's vicious attacks at the laboratory door. So far, however, the door held.

Midnight, who had been silent for the past minute, began to growl softly.

"We're all right," I said, patting his head. Midnight would never be able to win a fight with a velociraptor, but I was glad he was with us. He's very protective, and it was great to have a four-legged friend ready to help.

Near the laboratory door, Dr. Wentmeyer

had picked up the television remote and switched the channels until he found what he was looking for. On the monitor, a hallway appeared. In the hall, a velociraptor was charging. We watched the dinosaur lunge, and we heard the repercussion as the weight of his body hit the door.

Soon, however, the dinosaur realized he couldn't get through the door. If it had been wood, he probably would have succeeded. But the steel was just too strong for him to break through. On the monitor, we watched as he stormed down the hall in frustration.

Dr. Wentmeyer hurried to the time machine, pressed a button, and the panel door slid open.

"I'm going after him," he told us. "You two stay inside the time machine. I'm going to see if I can lure that velociraptor to me and put him to sleep with my electronic brain wave inhibitor."

"But what about the other velociraptor outside?" I asked.

"I'm sure he'll stay outside," the doctor said. "Right now, while they are separated, I have a chance to stop them both. If they are together, I wouldn't have a chance."

"If we're here in the time machine and something happens to you, how are we going to help you?" Kara asked.

"I'll be fine," Dr. Wentmeyer said, raising his electronic brain wave inhibitor. "I've got my secret weapon. He won't be able to hurt me. I'll try to find the one in the building first . . . then, we'll decide what to do with the one outside."

It sounded like a good plan. After all: Dr. Wentmeyer might be a little strange, but he was very, very smart.

He pressed a button on the outside panel, and the door slid closed. Kara, Midnight, and I were alone in the time machine.

"I sure hope he knows what he's doing," Kara said as we watched Dr. Wentmeyer. He glanced up at the television monitor to make sure the velociraptor wasn't in the hallway. Even when he reached the door, he opened it slowly and peered cautiously into the hall. Then, he slipped out of the laboratory.

On the television monitor, we watched Dr. Wentmeyer slink down the hall. He kept looking back over his shoulder to make sure the velociraptor wasn't approaching from behind.

"Look!" I said, pointing at the monitor.

The velociraptor had appeared at the end of the hall, in front of the doctor!

Thankfully, Dr. Wentmeyer saw it at the same time we did. He stopped, holding his electronic brain wave inhibitor in front of him.

The dinosaur stopped. He bobbed his head from side to side, sizing up his prey.

"The velociraptor is in for a surprise when he attacks," I said. "Watch. He's going to be out cold the minute he attacks the doctor."

Suddenly, there was a shattering of glass. Shiny shards fell like rain, sprinkling down in the hallway behind Dr. Wentmeyer.

The other velociraptor had leapt through the window and was now in the hall, behind Dr. Wentmeyer!

*There was nowhere he could go!*

We could only watch as Dr. Wentmeyer backed against the wall. His head snapped from left to right, watching each dinosaur. So far, the velociraptors made no move to attack. Rather, they just watched the doctor warily, as if they were waiting for just the right moment to strike.

"Oh, no!" Kara gasped. She covered her mouth with her hands. "He won't be able to fight both of them at the same time!"

On the television monitor, the velociraptors started to move. Their steps were very slow, and the creatures watched Dr. Wentmeyer carefully.

"We should have asked the doctor how to open the time machine door," I said. "Then, we could help him."

"What could *we* do?" Kara asked. "We don't have any way to defend ourselves, let alone help Dr. Wentmeyer."

"I don't know," I said, glancing at the control panel behind me. "But we can't just stand here and watch him get torn to pieces."

I turned to the control panel. "I wonder which one of these buttons opens the door," I said. I glanced quickly over my shoulder through the window at the television monitor hanging on the laboratory wall. The velociraptors were still moving toward the doctor. He was in the middle, and there was nowhere he could go. No matter which way he turned, he would have to face one of the vicious dinosaurs, and it wouldn't be long before they attacked. He might be able to stop one with his electronic brain wave inhibitor . . . but the remaining velociraptor would tear him apart.

I didn't know what to do . . . but I had to do *something*. I started pressing buttons on the control panel.

*I hope I don't accidentally send us back in time a billion years,* I thought.

"What are you doing?!?!" Kara asked.

"One of these buttons has to open the door!" I said. "I've got to get out of here and help Dr. Wentmeyer!"

I pressed a red button, and an alarm started ringing in the time machine, surprising us. I pressed it again, and the alarm died.

And on the television monitor on the other side of the laboratory, the velociraptors were getting closer and closer to the doctor.

I pressed a bunch of buttons—and the door suddenly slid open! I didn't even know what button I pushed that made it work . . . but it was open!

"Stay here!" I ordered Kara. "I'm going to open the door to see if I can distract one of the velociraptors!"

"Don't go into the hall!" Kara said.

"I won't!"

Midnight leapt out of the time machine, but I stopped him. "No," I said sternly. Then, I pointed into the time machine. "Stay with Kara!"

Reluctantly, Midnight walked back into the time machine and sat.

My plan was this: I was going to race to the laboratory door, throw it open, and yell. Hopefully, it would distract the dinosaurs. If one of them came after me, I could slam the door closed. It might give Dr. Wentmeyer time to zap one of the velociraptors with that electronic thingamabob he invented. Then, he'd be able to zap the other one. He wouldn't have to fight off both of them at the same time.

What I was going to do didn't sound all that dangerous . . . but there was something that I hadn't thought about.

And in less than ten seconds, my plan was about to go horribly wrong . . . .

I raced to the laboratory door and threw it open. I poked my head out and yelled.

*"Hey! You ugly reptiles! Come and get me!"*

I succeeded in getting the attention of the dinosaurs—but there was no sign of Dr. Wentmeyer!

Just then, Kara shouted.

"He went into another room!" she shouted. "He opened a door and went inside!"

Which was good news. After all: now Dr. Wentmeyer was safe.

But I wasn't.

The velociraptors saw me, and they didn't waste another second. They attacked, coming at me like speeding trains!

*"Brandon!"* Kara shouted. *"They're coming after you!"*

I'd already turned and started to run. I knew I'd be safe in the time machine, but there was one thing I wanted to get before I went back into the safety of the time machine: the television remote control. From inside the time machine, I would be able to switch channels and watch what was going on in and around the building. Maybe we would even be able to see where Dr. Wentmeyer was.

However, once again, I made a serious miscalculation. While I ran to the table to pick up the remote control, I didn't pay attention to the fact that the laboratory door hadn't closed all the way. I heard a dull thud, and after I snapped up the remote control, I turned.

What I saw made my blood chill.

One of the velociraptors had succeeded in getting his snout between the door and the doorjamb. He easily opened the door and wriggled through, followed by the other dinosaur.

*"Brandon!"* Kara screeched.

Midnight growled and snarled, but he remained in the time machine next to Kara.

And I bolted. I didn't even have a chance to pick up the remote control.

Both velociraptors came at me.

Now, I'm a fast runner . . . but was I fast enough to outrun two bloodthirsty velociraptors?

I was about to find out.

**25**

I nearly slipped on the tile floor as I ran. I was only about twenty feet from the door of the time machine, but the velociraptors were already on their way, and they were *fast!*

"*Hurry, Brandon, hurry!*" Kara screamed.

One step. Two. Three—

"*They're right behind you!*"

Suddenly, time seemed to stop as a memory came back to me. It was last spring, and I was on my bicycle, racing home from school. It's only a couple of miles from my house, and I usually ride my bike unless it's raining or it's cold. One day last year, we got snow, which is unusual in West Virginia.

On that particular day, I was racing my friend, Lamar Shoda, home. Lamar lives a few blocks from my house. He's pretty fast on his bike, too, and this time he was in the lead as we sped along the sidewalk. We had to stop at crosswalks and look for cars, of course . . . but when we got out of town, we turned onto Hemphill Road. It's a dirt road, wide, and there's usually not any traffic: the only cars or trucks you see are people who live on the street.

And it was here where we could really break away and pedal *fast* without having to stop. Plus, there's a steep hill on Hemphill Road. You can get going so fast down the hill that you don't even need to pedal. You just grip the handlebars, tuck down, and hold on.

Well, when we reached the hill, Lamar was still in front of me by about twenty feet. Halfway down, he stopped pedaling, and so did I. We were flying!

My plan was to wait until we'd reached the

bottom of the hill. Then, I was going to try and pass Lamar before he had a chance to pedal.

Things didn't work out that way.

The front tire of Lamar's bike hit a pothole. He lost control and sailed over the handlebars. He tumbled and rolled to the side, a flailing bundle of arms, elbows, knees, and feet.

His bike tumbled, too . . . directly into my path.

I was going too fast to try to turn—I'd wipe out for sure. The only thing I could do was hit my brakes hard and hope the bike tumbled out of my way. Both my tires locked up, and rubber skidded on dirt.

But, in the next split second, I realized that I wasn't going to avoid hitting Lamar's bike. Everything had happened so fast, but I now realized the inevitable: I was going to crash.

And crash I did! I hit Lamar's bike and went sailing over the handlebars, just like Lamar had done. I landed on my chest so hard the wind was knocked from me. I tumbled and rolled and banged every part of my body on the hard-packed ground. My backpack split open, and my homework—papers, pencils, and textbooks—flew out.

Thankfully, we weren't hurt, and it was a combination of luck and the fact we were both wearing our bike helmets. I'd hit my head hard, but the helmet had done its job.

But I always remembered that last final instant before I hit Lamar's tumbling bike, and the horror that I felt *knowing* I was going to hit it, that I was going down, that I was going to crash. Just thinking about it was enough to give me shudders.

Like now.

Despite the fact that I was racing to the open door of the time machine, I could hear the charging velociraptors right behind me. I could hear their screechy snarls and their claws scraping the tile.

And once again, that familiar horror overwhelmed me as I knew for certain there was going to be no escape. Not this time.

I wasn't going to make it to the time machine.

I tried.

Man, did I *ever*. I took a huge, bounding leap and tried to run faster, but the velociraptors were quicker. I tripped over my own feet . . . and went down.

Suddenly, I heard another growling sound, altogether different from the gravelly screeches of the velociraptors.

*Midnight!*

Usually, he is so obedient that he doesn't do anything unless I tell him. Moments before, I'd ordered him back into the time machine. But now that he knew I was really in danger, he was going to fight.

Just before one of the velociraptors was about to sink his teeth into my leg, Midnight was upon him. It was enough to divert the dinosaur's attention away from me, and I didn't waste any time. I pulled my leg away and sprang through the door of the time machine, tumbling to the floor in a heap, crashing into the wall on the other side. I was safe.

For Midnight, however, it was going to be a different story. I knew there was no way he would be able to take on *one* velociraptor, let alone *two*.

I got to my feet, horrified at the thought of losing my best friend. Midnight had just saved my life . . . and he was going to lose his.

However, he was fighting smart. Instead of attacking the dinosaurs, he snapped at them, then darted away when one of them lunged. He circled them, snarling and growling, snapping and yowling. The velociraptors lunged at him, but he was faster.

"Atta boy, Midnight!" I shouted.

"Shut the door!" Kara screamed. *"Shut the door!"*

"I'm not leaving my dog out there!" I replied.

"But they're going to get us!" she squealed.

*"My dog just saved my life!"* I shouted. *"I'm not leaving him!"*

Midnight was still circling the two dinosaurs, and it seemed the reptiles were getting madder and madder. They were trying to sink their teeth into him, but my dog was faster. And I'll admit it: I was really proud of him at that moment. He's always been a super-smart dog, and now he'd saved my life. Not only that, he was fighting two angry velociraptors and holding his ground.

While he battled the two dinosaurs, a movement on the television monitor on the wall caught my attention. I glanced up to see Dr. Wentmeyer. He had emerged from the room where he'd been hiding and was now hurrying down the hall toward the laboratory. In one hand, he was carrying his electronic whatchamacallit. In the other hand, he carried what looked to be a ball of clothing.

The next thing I knew, he had placed the tennis racquet-thing on the floor and was opening the door of the laboratory!

"Hey!" he shouted.

His voice caught the attention of the dinosaurs. Even Midnight snapped around in surprise, curious as to where the voice came from.

That was just what I needed. *"Midnight!"* I shouted. *"Here!"*

Midnight obeyed, darting around the dinosaurs. He bounded into the time machine and wagged his tail, as if this whole thing was just a game. He was probably having fun!

Meanwhile, the velociraptors had turned their attention to Dr. Wentmeyer and the wad of clothing he was carrying in his arms.

*How's he going to defend himself?* I wondered. *What's he going to do with a bunch of clothes? He's not going to be able to stop the dinosaurs with clothing!*

"*Come and get me!*" he suddenly shouted to the velociraptors.

And that's what they did. They attacked like

angry hornets . . . and Dr. Wentmeyer had nothing to defend himself.

He was about to become dinosaur food.

The two velociraptors lunged at the same time. I thought Dr. Wentmeyer was going to go into the hall and close the door, but he didn't. Instead, he spread his arms wide, revealing not a bundle of clothing—but a net!

Just before the dinosaurs reached him, he threw the net out. It draped over the two creatures like a sheet. They went down in a heap, their legs and arms caught in the web-like material.

And were they ever *mad!* Like the one trapped in the steel box on the other side of the room, the velociraptors in the net screeched and squealed. They thrashed about, lashing out with their sharp claws and teeth.

The question was: *what was the doctor going to do now?* He had them trapped—for the moment—in the net. I was sure it would only be a matter of minutes, or maybe even seconds, before the dinosaurs tore their way out.

However, Dr. Wentmeyer had already thought of that.

He was still holding the laboratory door open. Now, he knelt down and picked up the electronic whatever-he-called-it. He lowered it over the dinosaurs and flipped a switch on the handle.

The two velociraptors immediately fell silent. They stopped moving.

*"Good going!"* I shouted.

"We don't have much time," Dr. Wentmeyer said. "We've got to get them inside the time machine and get them back to their home in the past. Hurry!"

Kara and I bounded out of the time machine, and Midnight followed. We stopped and stared down at the two unconscious dinosaurs.

"I sure wish I had my camera," Kara said.

"I have one," Dr. Wentmeyer said. "But let's not worry about that now. Let's get these things in the time machine. I can operate it by remote control, and we can send them back to where they belong."

Kara and I knelt down, and so did Dr. Wentmeyer. We got to work untangling the net from the dinosaurs. The doctor had been lucky he used his electronic thing when he did, as the dinosaurs had already torn and chewed through many of the strands. In another few seconds, they would have freed themselves.

Still, it took nearly two full minutes to get them untangled, and we still had to get them into the time machine.

"One at a time," Dr. Wentmeyer said. "Let's drag them over and get them into the machine. Then, I can use my electronic brain wave inhibitor to subdue the one we have in the steel box. Once all three are in the machine, I can send them on their way."

Finally, it looked like our ordeal was about

over. Sure, it had been exciting, but it had been dangerous and scary. The only dinosaurs I ever wanted to see again were the ones in books and movies.

Of course, when you're dealing with ferocious dinosaurs, anything can happen . . . .

Dr. Wentmeyer and I dragged the first velociraptor to the time machine. I was surprised at how heavy he was. Although he was only twice the size of Midnight, he felt ten times heavier. I doubted the three of us would be able to pick him up.

But we didn't have to. We dragged his limp body across the floor and through the door of the time machine. Then, we did the same with the other. Midnight sniffed the creatures nervously, growling softly.

"Now," Dr. Wentmeyer said. "Let's get the

other one."

He picked up his electronic brain wave inhibitor and hurried to the other side of the room. Kara and I followed. Midnight, however, remained near the dinosaurs in the time machine, eyeing them suspiciously.

The velociraptor in the steel box had been silent, but when he heard us approaching, he started snarling and screeching.

"This is going to be a little tricky," Dr. Wentmeyer said. "The steel box will interfere with the waves sent off by this unit. We'll need to get the door open and the dinosaur away from the box before we can put him to sleep."

"Why don't we use the net?" I said. "It's not totally torn up. We can throw the net over him when we open the door. He'll get caught in it, and that'll give you enough time to zap him."

Dr. Wentmeyer's eyes widened, and he smiled. "Brilliant, boy, brilliant!" he said. "Go get the net!"

I ran around the time machine. Midnight was now seated on the laboratory floor, staring through the door of the machine, standing guard over the two velociraptors.

"Good boy," I said, and I patted his head as I walked past him. I picked up the net and wadded it into my arms. Then, I carried it across the room where Dr. Wentmeyer and Kara waited.

"How about if I stand on the box while you open it?" I asked the doctor. "Then, all I have to do is drop the net down on him."

"You'll have to be fast," Dr. Wentmeyer said. "As soon as I open the door, he's going to come charging out."

I stood on top of the steel box. The velociraptor beneath me seemed to sense this and became even more agitated.

I spread the netting out and held it up over the door.

"Kara," I said. "Get back. Just in case."

Kara took a few steps back and leaned against the time machine. "Hurry," she said, "before the other two wake up."

I looked at Dr. Wentmeyer, and he looked at me. He was holding his electronic brain wave inhibitor in front of him, ready to use it on the dinosaur.

"Ready?" he asked.

I nodded. "Yeah," I said.

He reached down, flipped a latch, and opened the door.

I knew the velociraptor was going to come racing out right away, so I dropped the net—but it fell to the floor in a heap! It should have caught the dinosaur . . . but he was still in the box!

I suddenly realized what he'd done. You have to remember that the velociraptor was one of the most intelligent of all dinosaurs. They were smart hunters and planners.

And this one had outsmarted us. He'd waited until the net hit the ground, where it wouldn't catch him . . . and then he suddenly burst out and attacked Dr. Wentmeyer, knocking him to the ground and sending the electronic brain wave inhibitor flying across the room!

The dinosaur pounced on Dr. Wentmeyer, who tried to roll away. The velociraptor snapped at him and caught his shirt in his jaws. The fabric tore easily—but at least it was his shirt and not his arm!

I sprang into action, leaping off the steel box. I grabbed the puddle of netting on the floor and picked it up. Then, I spread it out and held it in the air.

Dr. Wentmeyer was on his back on the floor. He grabbed one of the folding chairs and swung it in front of him. He was just in time, too, as the dinosaur was making another assault. The chair kept the velociraptor from sinking his teeth into Dr. Wentmeyer's arm.

"Move back!" I shouted.

Dr. Wentmeyer was able to get to his feet, and that was the chance I needed. It was risky, but I took a step toward the angry dinosaur, who now turned his attention toward me.

I dropped the netting on top of him before he could attack. He snapped with his jaws and slashed with his claws, but the net held him—at least momentarily.

Dr. Wentmeyer scrambled to his feet. He darted to where his electronic brain wave inhibitor had fallen, and he picked it up.

*"He's chewing through the net!"* I yelled. *"Hurry!"*

Dr. Wentmeyer rushed to the dinosaur, holding his invention in front of him. It was hard to believe he'd turned an ordinary tennis racquet into something that he was now using to put a dinosaur to sleep!

The velociraptor was madder than ever,

chewing the netting and slashing it apart. It wouldn't be long before he'd create a hole large enough for escape.

Dr. Wentmeyer flicked a switch on the handle, and a confused look came over his face. He flicked the switch again.

"It's . . . it's not working!" he said. "It must have been damaged when I dropped it!"

That alone was bad news. What was worse: at that moment, the velociraptor succeeded in chewing his way through the net. He was loose—and we had no way to defend ourselves!

Just when I thought things couldn't have gotten any worse, they had. A velociraptor was loose again.

I grabbed a metal folding chair. It wasn't much, but I might be able to use it to keep the dinosaur away from me.

Dr. Wentmeyer backed away as the velociraptor lunged at him. The beast screeched and squealed and went after the doctor's leg. Dr. Wentmeyer used his electronic brain wave inhibitor, poking it at the dinosaur to push him away. He succeeded, but the beast kept coming after him. Finally, the doctor climbed onto a table. This, however, only encouraged the velociraptor to leap. It crouched down and flew up into the air like a super-frog! Dr. Wentmeyer ducked down just in time. The velocirapter went soaring past, crashing into an old washing machine and knocking over a metal garbage can that was overflowing with debris.

Dr. Wentmeyer began fiddling with the racquet in his hands as the velociraptor stumbled and readied for another attack.

"I think I've got it working!" the doctor said. "Next time he attacks, I'll get him!"

The dinosaur attacked, all right. But this time, he went after *me!*

He charged at me like a rhinoceros: head down, legs thundering on the tile floor. I held the metal chair in front of me. Just as he made his final lunge, I leapt out of the way. He knocked the chair out of my hands, and it clanged to the floor.

And I wasn't going to take any chances. In two giant leaps, I was at the table Dr. Wentmeyer was standing on. I quickly climbed up and stood next to him. I was breathing hard, gasping for air. My heart clanged in my chest.

"Be ready to get out of the way," Dr. Wentmeyer said. "He's going to attack again. This time, I'll be able to use my electronic brain wave inhibitor."

Well, Dr. Wentmeyer was right. The velociraptor attacked again . . . but he didn't attack us.

*He went after Kara!*

Kara had been leaning against the other side of the time machine peering around the corner. I'd been so busy with Dr. Wentmeyer that I hadn't had the time to glance in her direction. Now, the velociraptor had spotted her . . . but she had nowhere to go. Even if she *tried* to run away, there was no way she would be faster than the dinosaur.

I did the only thing I could think of and shouted as loud as I could.

*"Hey!"*

I was hoping that my scream would get the

attention of the dinosaur and distract him for a moment. That might give Kara time to run. I had no idea where she would run to, but it would be better than just standing there and getting gobbled up by a dinosaur!

It worked, at least for the moment. The dinosaur turned and looked at me, and that gave Kara enough time to dart around to the other side of the time machine. But she didn't stop there. She ran straight to the laboratory door and went into the hall.

And the only reason the velociraptor didn't chase her?

*Midnight.*

He had been guarding the two sleeping velociraptors. Now, he appeared around the corner of the time machine. The hair on his back was raised. He was moving slowly, snarling and baring his teeth. I'd never seen him look so vicious, ever. Midnight is the sweetest dog in the world, but now that we were in real danger, he was going to put up the fight of his life. Even the velociraptor stopped. He seemed uncertain as to what to do. Now that he was the only dinosaur, he didn't seem so anxious to take on my dog. Not alone, anyway.

And Midnight kept coming toward him. Slowly, deliberately. He snarled and growled, and saliva dripped from his mouth. Clearly, he was ready for a fight.

But, after a moment, the velociraptor seemed to decide that Midnight wasn't going to be much of a threat to him. He began walking toward my dog.

A chill swept through me. I knew if the velociraptor and Midnight got into a fight, there would only be one winner.

And I knew who would lose.

Thankfully, Dr. Wentmeyer had already sprang into action. He carried his electronic brain wave inhibitor in front of him and walked toward the snarling, screeching reptile. When the velociraptor saw him, he turned . . . just as the doctor flipped the switch.

What happened next was really weird. The dinosaur's eyes rolled around. He stopped moving, and his jaw closed. He teetered this way and that and then fell to the tile in a heaping crash.

*"You did it!"* I shouted. *"You got him!"*

I was so excited about Dr. Wentmeyer zapping the velociraptor that I'd completely forgotten about the other two in the time machine . . . .

As soon as the velociraptor hit the floor, Dr. Wentmeyer placed his electronic brain wave inhibitor on the table.

"Help me drag him to the time machine!" he said.

I raced to his side. Together, we pulled the dinosaur across the tile and around to the front of the time machine.

Midnight began growling again.

"Shhh, buddy," I said. "It's okay. He's sleeping. He can't hurt us."

Midnight, however, continued to growl, snarling louder and louder.

Then, I heard a noise from inside the time machine. Dr. Wentmeyer and I looked up at the same time.

*The two velociraptors inside the time machine were waking up!*

I spun and ran back across the room, snapping up the doctor's electronic brain wave inhibitor. I tossed it to him, and he yanked it out of the air. He hustled into the time machine where the two dinosaurs were struggling to get to their feet. They were groggy and slow. Dr. Wentmeyer leaned over and held his electronic brain wave inhibitor above them. As soon as he turned it on, the velociraptors flopped to the floor, motionless once again.

"There," he said as he stepped out of the machine. He stopped at the sleeping dinosaur on the floor and placed his electronic brain wave inhibitor on a table. "Let's get this one in the machine and get them on their way."

I hurried back across the room and helped him drag the velociraptor into the time machine.

All the while, Midnight watched suspiciously, growling softly.

"Don't worry, Midnight," I said. "They'll be gone soon."

We dragged the dinosaur into the time machine.

"There," Dr. Wentmeyer said. He took a seat in front of the control panel in the time machine and began typing furiously at the keyboard while watching the monitor. All the while, he talked to himself.

"Okay . . . there . . . insert parallel molecular coordinates . . . yes . . . that's good—"

He paused and watched the screen for a moment. A long row of numbers suddenly popped up.

"There!" he said. "I've programmed the machine to open the door on its own. Once it reaches its destination back in time, the door will open automatically. The velociraptors will leave when they wake up, and the machine is programmed to return all by itself. All we need is the remote control."

He stepped out of the time machine and

walked to the desk where he'd placed the remote control. A confused look came over his face as he shuffled a few things around.

"What's the matter?" Kara asked.

"The remote was right here," he said. He began pawing through the pile of junk on a desk. "It must be here, somewhere," he said. "I've always kept it right here on this desk."

Kara and I hurried to the desk and helped the doctor find the remote control.

Suddenly, Dr. Wentmeyer looked on the floor. His jaw fell, and his eyes bulged.

*"No!"* he said as he knelt down. *"This is terrible! Awful!"*

What did he see?

I bent sideways and looked down. When I saw what the doctor was looking at, I knew that our ordeal with the velociraptors wasn't over yet.

The remote control had fallen to the floor. Several broken pieces, along with two small batteries, were scattered on the tile. Dr. Wentmeyer picked each one up, then stood. He looked very somber.

"If the remote control doesn't work," he said quietly, "we won't be able to operate the time machine and return the velociraptors to the Cretaceous period."

He began piecing together the small remote control.

"Do you think you'll be able to make it

work?" I asked.

"We'll know in a minute," he replied.

"It better be a fast minute," Kara said. "Those velociraptors aren't going to be asleep for too long."

Dr. Wentmeyer worked on the remote for a little bit longer. Finally, he aimed it at the time machine and pressed a button.

Nothing happened.

Dr. Wentmeyer shook his head. "It's no use," he said. "It's not working. I'll have to make another remote control, but we don't have the time. Those dinosaurs are going to wake up at any moment."

"Well, at least they're in the time machine," I said. "They can't get out, can they?"

Dr. Wentmeyer shook his head. "No, I don't think they can. But they'll probably destroy the control panel. That means they'll be stuck here, in our time period."

"Is there anywhere else we can take them?" I asked. "What if we took them out and dragged them to another room? You and I can drag the dinosaurs, one at a time. Kara can carry your brain wave-thingy, and when one of them begins to wake up, you can just put them to sleep again."

Dr. Wentmeyer's eyes lit up. "You know," he said, "that might just work! We can drag them across the hall and into my storage room. They might tear it up, but there are no windows in it, so they can't get outside. And it's a steel door, one like my laboratory has. I don't think they'd be able to break it down. And it might give me time to repair this remote control or make another one."

Kara rolled her eyes. "I think I know what's wrong with the remote control," she said, and she pointed to the table.

*How on earth would Kara know how to fix the remote control?* I thought. However, when I looked where she was pointing, I realized she was probably right.

# 34

*The batteries for the remote control were still on the table! Dr. Wentmeyer had forgotten to put them back!*

"Oh, for goodness sakes!" he said, slapping the palm of his hand to his forehead. "I can't believe I did that!"

Dr. Wentmeyer picked up the two batteries and put them in the remote. After fiddling with it for a moment, he aimed it at the time machine. He pressed a button, and we heard a noise.

"Success!" he said.

We heard a hum—the same one we'd heard when we'd traveled back in time—and it grew louder and louder. Dr. Wentmeyer pressed a few more buttons on the remote control.

"Step back a little," he said, and we followed him to the far side of the room.

"Come here, Midnight," I said, and he trotted across the floor, tongue hanging out and tail wagging.

The hum grew louder still, until it was nearly deafening.

"It won't be long now," Dr. Wentmeyer said loudly. He had to nearly shout to be heard over the continuous whirring sound.

And I wondered what was going to happen. Before, when we'd been inside the time machine, we couldn't see outside until we'd actually reached a destination. From the outside, I was curious as to what we'd see.

Dr. Wentmeyer pressed another button on the remote control. "There," he said. "Time to send those nasty critters back to where they belong."

"We forgot to take pictures!" Kara said.

I hadn't thought about that. Sure, it was

disappointing, but at least we were alive. Still, it would have been cool to have some pictures to show our friends. Without pictures, no one in the world would believe us if we told them that we saw real, live dinosaurs from eighty-three million years ago!

"It's working perfectly!" the doctor said, clearly pleased with himself and his invention. "Watch!"

At first, nothing seemed to be happening. We could hear the loud droning, but there was nothing to see except the large, black time machine.

Then, something *did* happen.

The entire time machine began to blur. It changed from black to a misty gray. Then, it began to shimmer, and the entire thing turned into a cloud. It didn't even appear to be solid anymore, but more like a dense swarm of insects. Soon, the entire contraption looked like static on television. It was incredible to watch.

"What's it doing?" Kara asked.

"That's how the machine travels through time," Dr. Wentmeyer said. "Of course, it's all very complicated. But it's almost finished. It should be returning any moment now."

"That fast?" I asked. "But it hasn't been two minutes since you pressed the button."

"Remember: time travel is very different from ordinary travel. The machine isn't moving distances the way we would ordinarily think. It is moving through space and time."

Which was still pretty confusing, if you ask me.

The dense cloud began to thicken . . . but another shape appeared on top of it—something that didn't seem to be part of the machine.

Dr. Wentmeyer frowned, and his face grew serious. He watched the machine curiously.

*"What is that?!?!"* Kara shouted, pointing to the top of the time machine.

"It's another velociraptor!" Dr. Wentmeyer shouted. "One of them came back on the top of the machine!"

By now, the time machine looked as it once had—a big, black box—with an angry velociraptor that suddenly leapt from the top of the machine and lunged at us!

# 35

*"Out the door! Quick!"* Dr. Wentmeyer shouted.

*"Midnight!"* I shouted. *"This way!"*

The three of us raced to the door, followed by Midnight. Kara reached it first and threw it open, and we bounded into the hall. Midnight was right behind me. I was glad he hadn't challenged the dinosaur.

Dr. Wentmeyer slammed the door shut just in time. The velociraptor crashed into it. Through the window, we watched him as he backed away. He watched us warily. Then, he attacked the door again.

"He knows we're out here, but he can't get to us," Dr. Wentmeyer said.

We could hear the velociraptor moving around the laboratory, crashing into things.

"Now what do we do?" I asked. "Your electronic thing is in there, so you can't put him to sleep."

Dr. Wentmeyer thought for a moment. Finally, he spoke.

"Step back," he said. Kara and I did as he asked. Then, he opened the laboratory door a tiny crack. He raised the remote control, aimed it at the time machine, and pressed a button. The door of the machine slid open.

Through the tiny crack, we saw that the velociraptor had stopped. He'd heard the door of the time machine open, and he walked cautiously toward it.

*"I'm hoping he's curious enough to step inside,"* the doctor whispered. "If he does, I can close the door, and we can send him back in time."

"But what if another one comes back?" I asked.

"We'll be ready, next time," Dr. Wentmeyer said.

We watched as the dinosaur approached the time machine. He stalked carefully, watching the machine for any movement. When he reached the door, he poked his head in and sniffed.

*"He smells the other dinosaurs,"* Dr. Wentmeyer said.

Then, the velociraptor did exactly what we were hoping for: he took a step inside the time machine. Dr. Wentmeyer waited with the remote control. When the dinosaur was completely inside, he pressed a button.

*The door closed, trapping the dinosaur!*

"You did it!" Kara said as Dr. Wentmeyer pushed the door open. He stepped into the laboratory and pressed a couple more buttons on the remote. The loud humming began again. We watched as the time machine turned into a gray mist that spun and whirled, just as it had done moments before.

Dr. Wentmeyer opened the laboratory door. "Stay in the hall," he said. He hurried through the laboratory and retrieved his electronic brain wave inhibitor from the table. Then, he backed away from the whirling time machine, waiting.

After a minute, the loud droning began to fade and the mist began to clear. Soon the time machine was solid again.

And the good news was there was no passenger on top!

Still, Dr. Wentmeyer wasn't taking any chances. He pressed a button on the remote control, and the door to the time machine opened. Cautiously, he stepped forward and peered inside, making sure there were no dinosaurs waiting. Then, he looked back at us.

"All clear," he said, and he returned his electronic brain wave inhibitor to the table.

I let out a sigh of relief as I pushed open the door. We strode into his laboratory.

"I have a few adjustments to make before I inform the world of my new invention," Dr. Wentmeyer said.

"Yeah," Kara said as she looked around the room. "And you might want to pick up around here before you invite anyone over."

As the saying goes: all's well that ends well.

Our ordeal with the velociraptors was over. We'd had the opportunity to do something no one else had ever done: travel back in time to see what it was like millions of years ago. We saw dinosaurs—velociraptors—up close. Almost *too* close. Still, I was excited for Dr. Wentmeyer and his invention. He was going to be world-famous, for sure.

And Dr. Wentmeyer told us not to worry about washing the windows and cleaning up around the outside of his laboratory. He said we'd helped him enough, and that we'd done enough work to pay for the broken window. We said good-bye, and he told us we were welcome to come back anytime. He again mentioned that he had some work to do on his time machine, but he invited us to try it out again.

"That would be fun," I said. "But let's stay away from dinosaurs."

At dinner, I told Mom and Dad everything that happened. I told them about Dr. Wentmeyer's time machine and how we'd tried to travel back in time to see Abraham Lincoln give his Gettysburg Address, but the machine messed up and sent us back eighty-three million years. I told them about the velociraptors and how they had hitched a ride back to the present day.

Just as I suspected, they didn't believe a single word. Dad just laughed. Mom listened, but she rolled her eyes in disbelief. "Honestly, Brandon," she said. "I don't know where you get your crazy stories."

"Next time, bring back a brontosaurus," Dad said with a wide grin. "I hear they're pretty tasty on the grill."

"You watch," I said. "Dr. Wentmeyer and his invention are going to be world-famous."

After dinner, I rode my bike over to Kara's house. Our plan was to ride to an open field a couple of miles away, where we could practice hitting a softball without breaking any windows.

When I got to Kara's house, her mom told me that she'd already left—which was strange. I headed down the street on my bike with my catcher's mitt looped over the handlebars. Far up ahead, I saw her on the side of the road. Her bike was on its kickstand and she was kneeling, looking at something on the side of the road. When I got closer, she saw me coming and shouted.

"*Brandon!*" she exclaimed, pointing to the ground at her feet. "*There are dinosaur footprints all over the place!*"

I slowed my bike, letting her words sink in. *Dinosaur footprints?!?!* I thought. *That can only mean that somehow, more dinosaurs had traveled through time . . . and they were on the loose!*

I began pedaling faster until I skidded to a stop next to Kara. I leapt off my bike.

"Where?!?!" I said. My eyes darted back and forth, searching the ground. "Where are the tracks?!?!"

"Right there!" she said, pointing to the tracks in the dirt. Then, she looked up and smiled.

I frowned and shook my head. "Those aren't dinosaur tracks," I said. "Those are just dog tracks.

Probably from Midnight."

"I know," Kara said with a laugh. "I was just kidding." She stood and got on her bike. "Ready to practice?"

"Yeah," I said. "We've still got a couple of hours before it gets dark."

It took us about ten minutes to bike to the field. It was a big, open space, surrounded by thick pine trees. The grass was nearly six inches high. There were a couple of trees in the field, but no houses. We wouldn't be breaking any windows!

But there was also something else:

*A person.*

There was a girl wandering in the field. She had shoulder-length brown hair and was wearing a gray sweater and blue jeans.

We stopped our bikes.

"Who's that?" I asked.

Kara shook her head. "I don't know," she replied. "I don't recognize her."

When the girl turned and saw us, she stopped. Then, she walked toward us.

"Hi," I said.

"Hi," the girl replied. "Is this your property?"

"No," I said. "We're just here to play softball. Do you live around here?"

The girl shook her head. "No, I'm just visiting my aunt. I live in New Hampshire."

"I'm Brandon, and this is Kara," I said.

"I'm Hannah," the girl said.

"We were just going to practice hitting the softball," I said. "You want to play?"

"Sure," Hannah said.

Turns out, Hannah was a pretty good pitcher. Not as good as Kara, but she was still quite good. We played for a long time—until the sun sank below the trees and the sky darkened.

And Hannah began to get nervous. She didn't say so, but I could tell that something was bothering her. I saw her look into the woods where it was growing dark quickly. Her eyes scoured the shadows, as if she were looking for something.

Kara pitched the ball, and I smacked it a good one. It sailed up over the field and landed near the edge of the forest. Hannah was in the outfield, using my mitt. The ball went way over her head, and she started after it. However, when she saw it land by the forest, she stopped. Then, she turned and looked at us, then back at the dark forest.

"What's wrong?" I called out.

"I'm afraid," Hannah replied meekly.

"Of what?" Kara asked.

Hannah still didn't go after the ball. Instead, she walked toward us.

"Ghosts," she said, glancing over her shoulder.

"Ghosts?" I replied. "There's no such thing as ghosts."

"You can believe what you want," Hannah said, "but I know ghosts are real."

"Have you seen one?" Kara asked.

Hannah nodded. "In New Hampshire."

I didn't believe her. "A *real* ghost?" I said. "How do you know?"

"Because I was there," Hannah said firmly. "And I *know* what I saw."

"Tell us," Kara said. She seemed fascinated.

"Okay," Hannah said. "But I'm warning you right now: what happened to us was pretty scary."

Well, *Hannah* might have been frightened

by something that happened to her in New Hampshire, but I knew there were no such things as ghosts.

I was *positive*.

But, as I listened, I became mesmerized by Hannah's story. Horrified, in fact, as she explained the terrifying things she went through earlier that summer in New Hampshire . . . .

# Next:

America's #1 Series for MAXIMUM Chills!

# #24: Haunting in New Hampshire

# Continue on for a FREE preview!

If you had asked me a year ago if I believed in ghosts, I would have said, in one word:

*No.*

Sure, I know lots of people believe they've seen ghosts, but I'm not one of them. I like to read ghost stories, but even when I was little I was never afraid of ghosts. I used to be afraid of monsters under my bed or in my closet, but that was when I was very young. There are no monsters in closets or under the bed, just like there is no such thing as ghosts. And I wasn't afraid of them.

All that changed one horrifying summer, when we moved into a bigger house on the other side of the city.

My name is Hannah Bayford, and I live in Concord, New Hampshire. Concord is the state capital. I have one brother named Clay. I'm twelve, and he's eight. He's a lot of fun to hang around with . . . most of the time. But he does a lot of things that gross me out. He catches frogs and puts them in his pocket. Toads, too. He used to catch worms and put them in his pocket. One time he forgot about it and Mom found them when she was doing the laundry. She totally freaked out! It was actually pretty funny . . . but Mom got mad. Clay doesn't put worms in his pocket anymore.

We moved for a couple of reasons. Number one, Mom has always said she wanted a bigger house. And number two, Dad has always wanted to move away from the city to somewhere that wasn't so busy. I thought that would be cool. I like the forest, and I thought it would be fun to be able to wander among tall trees and build forts with my brother.

So, beginning in the spring, we started house-hunting. Every weekend we would go for a drive and look at houses that were for sale. We looked at a lot of houses. Some of them were big, but Mom and Dad said they hadn't found one that was perfect.

Until one gray, rainy, Saturday afternoon.

Looking back, I should have known something was wrong. I should have known right away that the house we saw at the end of Cedar Mill Street wasn't what it appeared to be. Something told me right away—a little voice in my head—to stay away from the old house surrounded by huge, lofty trees.

Someone seemed to whisper in my ear:

*Don't go inside. Don't go near that house.*

But did I listen?

*Don't go inside. Don't go near that house.*

Nope. I told that little voice to go away, that it was just my imagination.

Very soon, however, I'd be wishing I'd listened to that voice. In fact, there was something that happened that very day—the day we first saw the house—that should have told all of us to stay away.

And it all started when we explored a room at the end of the hallway on the second floor of the house . . . .

We'd been driving around for about an hour. Rain had been falling most of the morning, and the roads were shiny and slick. An iron-gray sky loomed low, and mist hung in the air like smoke.

Mom spotted the 'HOUSE FOR SALE' sign first. It was orange and black, the kind you see for sale in department stores. There was a hand-drawn black arrow pointing to the right.

"There's something, right there," Mom said, and Dad turned the car onto Cedar Mill Street. We saw several houses, but they weren't very close together. They were old and big, too . . . at least twice the size of the house we were living in. The yards were large expanses of deep green grass. Huge trees, their gray and black trunks glossy from the rain, stood silent and still, sleeping in the morning drizzle. Rain dripped from sagging, green leaves.

"I wonder which house is for sale?" Mom said as our car crawled down the deserted street. We continued until the road came to a dead end. Here, a tall, two-story house loomed behind several enormous, old trees. It seemed almost hidden behind branches and leaves.

And there was a big sign in the yard that read: 'FOR SALE BY OWNER.'

"This is the place," Dad said, and he pulled the car into the driveway. He stopped in front of an attached two-car garage.

I looked up at the big, old house—and that's when I first heard the faint voice in my head.

*Don't go inside. Don't go near that house.*

Oh, I knew it was only my imagination getting to me. The house looked a little creepy in with the gray sky and the rain, but it wasn't scary looking or anything. The house was old, but it was in good shape. Someone had taken good care of it. It looked like it had a fresh coat of white paint, and the rain made it glisten. Even the black shingles on the roof seemed to shine.

"Nice place," Dad said.

"I wonder if anyone is home," Mom said.

The car idled quietly, and rain tapped on the roof and windows.

*Don't go inside. Don't go near that house.*

There was that voice again. Sure, I knew it was only in my head. I knew it was my own voice.

But why? We'd looked at over a dozen homes in the past couple of months. Why did I have that strange gnawing of doom in my head? What was different about this house?

Lots . . . and I was about to find out why.

"Wait here," Dad said as he opened the door and stepped into the rain. He walked quickly to the covered porch and rang the doorbell.

"It sure is a big house," Clay said.

The front door opened, and a man appeared. He had gray hair and glasses. He and my dad began talking, but we couldn't hear what they were saying. The old man nodded several times, smiled, then closed the door. Dad jogged back to the car and got inside.

"He says we can come inside and take a look around," he said as he turned the key in the ignition. The car engine died.

"We have to go out in the rain?" Clay complained.

"You're not going to melt," I said. "Besides: all we have to do is run to the front door."

I pushed open the car door and stepped out. Clay climbed out my side. Mom and dad got out, too, and the four of us hurried to the porch. The front door opened, as if automatically. The old man appeared again, standing aside.

"Come in, come in!" he said. "I don't get visitors very often. Come in out of this rainy, cold weather!"

Upon entering, there were several things I noticed right away. First of all, we were in a spacious living room. The floor was made of dark brown wood, with even darker grains that looked like hair fibers. It was shiny, like it was covered with a layer of glass. There were several large, colorful rugs placed about, including one very big one centered in the living room. On the other side, a real fire burned real wood in a real fireplace. We have a fireplace in our home, but it burns gas and the logs are fake. All you have to do is flick a switch and poof! You have a fire. But *this* fire was real, and I could smell the musky odor of burnt wood. It made the room feel cozy and homey.

There was a large, fluffy black couch and two equally puffy reclining chairs, also black. They were so big and soft they looked like they would swallow you and trap you forever. A white cat was nestled on the arm of one of them. He was sleeping, and didn't even know we were there. Behind one of the couches, a staircase went up. Like the floor, the steps were made of dark wood, all glossy and shiny.

I counted twelve pictures hanging from the walls. They were all portraits, and they all looked to be very old. The pictures were black and white, but several had turned a dirty yellow over the years.

The old man closed the door.

"That awful rain," he said. "It hasn't stopped since Thursday. However, I heard that it's supposed to stop this morning and we might even see a little sunshine this afternoon."

"Thanks for letting us in to take a look around," Dad said. He started to take off his shoes, but the old man stopped him.

"No, no," he said, shaking his head. "Keep your shoes on. Be comfortable. A little rain or dirt won't hurt this old house. She's seen much worse over the years. Can I bring either of you some tea?"

"That would be nice," Mom said.

"Sure," Dad said. "That sounds good on a rainy day like today."

The old man smiled. "Good, good," he said. Please: feel free to look around, anywhere you wish." He looked at me, then at Clay. His eyes twinkled. "And you two might want to go upstairs," he said with a widening grin. "There is a certain room at the end of the hall I think you will find most interesting." He winked, then he looked at Mom. "Be right back with your tea." He turned, walked across the living room, and vanished into what appeared to be the kitchen.

"Let's go upstairs," I said to Clay.

"Don't touch a single thing," Mom warned. "Remember: we are guests in this house."

"Don't worry," I said. "We won't."

Clay and I walked across the living room and around the recliner and the sleeping cat. He woke up and looked at us curiously, like he'd never seen a human before. Then, he tucked his nose in his paws and closed his eyes.

The stairs creaked beneath our feet as we walked upstairs. The smell of wood smoke faded.

"I wonder how old this place is," Clay said.

"I don't know," I replied. "But it's *old*. Probably older than Grandpa."

At the top of the steps, a long hall opened up. Two glass chandeliers—like swarms of glittering diamonds—burned from the ceiling. Like everything else in the home, they, too, looked very old.

There were several doors on either side of the hall. All were closed. The end of the hall was capped with yet another door. It, too, was closed.

Downstairs, I heard Mom and Dad talking with the old man. He introduced himself, but by then, we were halfway down the hall and I couldn't hear what he said.

And a strange thing happened as we walked toward the door at the end of the hall. It seemed to grow darker all around us, like a cloud slipping under the sun. I looked up at the glowing chandeliers, but they seemed to be just as bright as ever. The air became cooler, too, and I wondered if there was a window open somewhere.

We reached the door at the end of the hall and stopped. The door wasn't closed all the way, and I could see a thin blade of darkness beyond the door and the frame.

The doorknob was faded brass, the color of a weathered penny. It had curious designs and patterns engraved over it. Clay reached out, but before he grasped it, he stopped suddenly.

We heard a squeak—and the door began opening . . . *all by itself!*

# ABOUT THE AUTHOR

Johnathan Rand is the author of more than 50 books, with well over 2 million copies in print. Series include **AMERICAN CHILLERS, MICHIGAN CHILLERS, FREDDIE FERNORTNER, FEARLESS FIRST GRADER**, and **THE ADVENTURE CLUB.** He's also co-authored a novel for teens (with Christopher Knight) entitled **PANDEMIA.** When not traveling, Rand lives in northern Michigan with his wife and two dogs. He is also the only author in the world to have a store that sells only his works: **CHILLERMANIA!** is located in Indian River, Michigan. Johnathan Rand is not always at the store, but he has been known to drop by frequently. Find out more at:

**www.americanchillers.com**

# ATTENTION YOUNG AUTHORS!
## DON T MISS

### JOHNATHAN RAND'S

# AUTHOR QUEST

## THE DEFINITIVE WRITER'S CAMP
## FOR SERIOUS YOUNG WRITERS

If you want to sharpen your writing skills, become a better writer, and have a blast, Johnathan Rand's Author Quest is for you!

Designed exclusively for young writers, Author Quest is 4 days/3 nights of writing courses, instruction, and classes at Camp Ocqueoc, nestled in the secluded wilds of northern lower Michigan. Oh, there are lots of other fun indoor and outdoor activities, too . . . but the main focus of Author Quest is about becoming an even better writer! Instructors include published authors and (of course!) Johnathan Rand. No matter what kind of writing you enjoy: fiction, non-fiction, fantasy, thriller/horror, humor, mystery, history . . . this camp is designed for writers who have this in common: they LOVE to write, and they want to improve their skills!

For complete details and an application, visit:

## www.americanchillers.com

Join the official

# AMERICAN
# CHILLERS

## FAN CLUB!

Visit www.americanchillers.com for details!

Johnathan Rand travels internationally for school visits and book signings! For booking information, call:

# 1 (231) 238-0338!

**www.americanchillers.com**

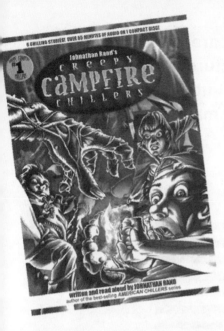

**All AudioCraft books are proudly printed, bound, and manufactured in the United States of America, utilizing American resources, labor, and materials.**

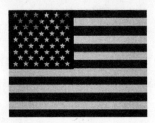

USA